W9-CPQ-824

THE WORLD OF THE PHARAOHS

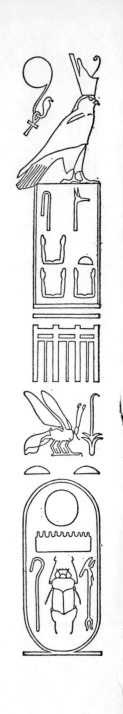

THE WORLD OF THE

PHARAOHS

BY HANS BAUMANN

Colour photographs by Albert Burges

Line drawings by Hans Peter Renner

PANTHEON BOOKS • 1960

Translated by Richard and Clara Winston

First published 1959 under the title *Die Welt der Pharaonen*
by Sigbert Mohn Verlag, Gütersloh, Germany.

Copyright © Sigbert Mohn Verlag 1959.
English translation copyright © 1960
by Pantheon Books Inc., 333 Sixth Avenue, New York 14, N.Y.,
and Oxford University Press, London, England.
Colour plates printed in Germany by
Mohn & Co. GmbH, Gütersloh, Germany.
Library of Congress Catalog Card Number: 60–11491
Manufactured in the United States of America
by H. Wolff Book Mfg. Co., New York, N.Y.

Fifth Printing, September 1966

CONTENTS

LIST OF TEXT ILLUSTRATIONS

LIST OF COLOUR PLATES

THE ANSWERER

The Nile pointed directly towards the sun. It was noon—the best
time of day for what Megdi had in mind. At home he had said that
he would take the tram from Cairo out to Giza to meet his father.
But it was still much too early for his father to be finished with his
work, so Megdi set out on his secret mission. He passed the camel
drivers and dragomans who lay in wait for tourists from all over
the world, and quickly left behind the road that led up to the eleva-
tion in the desert on which the pyramids stood. Soon he reached the
sharply drawn dividing line between the black and the red earth,
the tillable soil, and the sand. He was on the brink of the desert.

He looked out over the wasteland of tombs that surrounded the
pyramids. Never before had he set foot in this region without his
father. But today he was drawn irresistibly toward one of the shafts
which his father had always carefully avoided.

Megdi peered toward the Great Pyramid. On the south side of it
lay the two newly discovered royal ships, in chambers hewn out of
the rock. While building a road, an engineer named Kamal el Mallakh had come across forty-two limestone blocks jointed together

in a long row. Two days later the first block, weighing some twenty tons, had been lifted out. Mallakh had looked into the chamber and seen a fifty-foot-long barge whose bow was shaped like a lotus flower. An aura of fine perfume had risen from the five-thousand-year-old vessel. The newspapers of the world had printed lengthy accounts of the find, and now for a year experts had been busy examining the big boat and restoring it to its probable original form.

One of those experts was Megdi's father. He had brought home photographs of the royal barge, but he had forbidden Megdi to enter the chamber. And he was not one of those fathers who would change a "No" to a "Yes" for any amount of persistent pleading. Altogether, Megdi felt that his father was being rather hard on him. Last year Zakaria Ghoneim, leader of the excavations in nearby Saqqara, had discovered both an alabaster sarcophagus and a "new Pharaoh," but Megdi had not been taken along to see these either. He fretted because he had been excluded from the two most important discoveries of recent years.

Megdi's father was a man who was always sent for when something extraordinary came to light in the Land of the Nile. He was responsible for discoveries that were now displayed in the museum. Secretly, Megdi was proud of his father. But ever since the buried ships had been found, Megdi had begun prowling restlessly. It was

Egyptian boat with lotus-shaped bow

continually on his mind that Mallakh had found them by chance. Many other discoveries had been made by lucky finders who were not thinking of discovering anything. Once a young woman carrying a stack of books from one excavator's barracks to another had broken through into an underground chamber—on a path that she had walked over hundreds of times. Near the Valley of the Kings a horse had plunged its forefoot into an important grave, and once a donkey had stumbled with all four legs into a rich site. Why should not a boy who wanted to be an excavator hit on something important, if only he started looking hard? In the long run, Megdi thought, it was annoying to receive everything at second hand. To dig where no one had ever dug before him; to see something that no one had ever looked upon; to find a corridor that no one else knew about, not even his father—this was what Megdi thought about day and night. Now he had made up his mind to take the first step.

The area was guarded, but Megdi knew that in the midday heat even the gaffers dozed in their huts. It was the hour when all living things seemed to stop breathing.

He went on. For a few hundred paces he stayed on the borderline between the grass and sand, his left foot in the tilled land, his other on ground where not a blade of green grew. The soil, which had been flooded by the Nile, bore him with springy resilience, while the sand yielded treacherously underfoot. As soon as Megdi saw that a sand dune hid him from the small guard hut, he turned into the desert.

The opening of the shaft yawned before him, a square of blackness. He switched on his flashlight and aimed it into the shaft. A feeble glow of light struck the bottom. Megdi took off his shoes and hid them under sand; then he began climbing down. At first it was easy. With fingers and toes he felt for supports. The shaft was more than a yard wide from wall to wall. The window of light above him shrank. After Megdi had climbed down some fifty feet, he peered below him. For a moment he was frightened—there was still no bottom to be seen. He felt a quivering in his knees. But he knew that at the moment there was no turning back. Without looking up again, he continued his descent. From the lower rim of the shaft to the ground the distance was little higher than a table. Megdi jumped. Two tunnels scarcely wider than the shaft led north and south. Megdi decided on the southern passage. Stooping, he followed slowly after the feeble glow of his flashlight. Everything down here was silent as the light, as the sand underfoot. Not a sound penetrated; the desert extended even to this depth. Sand was everywhere.

The tunnels became so low that Megdi could proceed no farther without crawling. Suddenly there was a piece of wood in front of his nose. He grasped it. It crumbled under his touch, its paint flaking off. Looking closer, he realized that it was an ankh, a looped cross. Such crosses were painted on all sarcophagi in ancient times. They were regarded as the key to life. Abruptly, Megdi real

 *Ankh, the symbol of life*

ed that he was in the "Land of the Western Ones," as his father alled it—the realm of the dead. The thought did not disturb him 1 the slightest, for discoveries could be expected only where the ead had their dwellings. He thrust the painted piece of wood into is pocket. The roof of the passage rose slightly and Megdi was ble to move forward without effort. Then a spacious hall opened p, its floor a hollow some thirteen feet deep. The hollow was like a lried-up lake in which dry brooks from all four sides came to an nd. Megdi crossed the stone rim and crawled into the nearest pasageway. He came to a spot where a stone sarcophagus protruded rom the sand. The lid was missing. Hastily, Megdi scooped out he inside of the sarcophagus. He found nothing but sand. Disappointed, he crawled across it and soon came upon a half-buried porter's basket. With considerable difficulty he managed to pull it put of the sand. A tiny figure of burnt clay appeared, scarcely onger than a finger. As if it were necessary to hide it from the eyes of others, Megdi instantly tucked it into his pocket. In his pleasure over the find he forgot that he was at a spot where others had already tried their luck. Placing the flashlight so that its full beam fell upon the area in front of him, he dug without haste, leaning far down into the hollow. Behind him a small mound of sand rose.

Suddenly a hand touched his back. Megdi whirled around. In the dim light he saw an old face. It was not the face of any of the gaffers Megdi knew. The stranger held the boy with his eyes. Megdi felt for his flashlight. But the stranger had already seized it, and sent a cone of light gliding across the ceiling. Overhead Megdi saw a network of cracks.

"Stay close behind me!" the old man ordered in a muted voice,

15

as if he feared that any loud word might bring the ceiling dow
upon them. They crawled back. In narrow passages the ma
flashed the light behind him.

As soon as they reached the shaft, Megdi tried to climb ou
But he felt so stunned that he could not make headway. Th
stranger kneeled in order to help the boy into the shaft. When th
boy had clambered on his shoulders, he straightened up. The firs
twenty feet or so Megdi climbed without aid. But then he had n
choice; he had to seek support on the old man's shoulders agair
and was pushed up the shaft bit by bit. At the top, the bright ligh
struck savagely at Megdi. He was so exhausted that he had to si
down. The old man sat down in the sand beside him. Megdi threv
a timid look at the tall figure wrapped in a *galabia* that was a
bright a blue as the noonday sky. Under the strip of white clotl
wound around his head, the man's face stood out like dark wood
How, Megdi puzzled, had this old man had the strength to hel
him out of the shaft? Crestfallen, he looked down at his bare
scraped knees.

The man broke the silence. "As luck would have it I saw yo
disappear," he said without reproach. "Did you find anything, b
the way?"

Shamefacedly, Megdi took the little figure out of his pocket.

"Well, not too bad—an *ushabti,*" the old man said. And whe
Megdi looked inquiringly at him, he explained: "An answerer. Som
mummies had an *ushabti* for every day in the year." He took th
little figure from Megdi's hand and pointed to the writing whicl
began under the crossed arms and covered a good half of the littl
man. To Megdi's astonishment, this strange old fellow read th

16

hieroglyphics without effort: " 'When I am called to a task that must be done in the Land of the Western Ones, answer thou in my place: "Here am I." ' Every person of prominence made a point of having as many answerers as possible in his tomb. That is the reason thousands upon thousands of the little figures have been found."

"I would have found something better if I'd looked longer," Megdi said sulkily.

"Lucky it was only an *ushabti*," the old man replied, his eyes fixed unwaveringly upon the boy's face. "By the way, did you know that this past year two prowlers were buried under a collapsing roof in the chamber we just crossed?"

Ushabti

Megdi started.

"Sometimes the dead defend themselves," the old man declared calmly. "Not far from here a ransacked sarcophagus was found with the mummy and the robber lying in each other's arms. The ceiling of the tomb must have collapsed at the moment the plunderer was about to drag the mummy out of his coffin."

Megdi spoke up at last. "But I want to find something like my . . ." He suppressed the last word.

"So you should," the old man agreed. "Only as an excavator, not a robber who plays into Death's hands."

"I don't understand you," Megdi said.

"Look at the little answerer you found," the old man said. "Does he answer you?"

"Of course not. He can't."

"But he could have done so," the old man said earnestly. "When you took him from the place where he had lain for thousands of years, you took his voice from him. Now he is just one *ushabti* among thousands. But he was once the *ushabti* of a particular man; he could tell us something about that man, along with the other finds in the tomb. You have treated him as if he belonged to no one. Now he can no longer speak. And yet your father thinks the world of you."

"Do you know my father?" Megdi asked in alarm.

"I know all the archaeologists on the Nile," the old man declared. "And all of them know me."

"Who are you?" Megdi asked in mounting surprise.

"Gurgar."

"Gurgar!" Megdi burst out. "*The* Gurgar—who was present

18

when the Golden Pharaoh was discovered—Tutankhamen?"

"It was only natural for Carter to send for me," the old man said. "You see, I come from a place near the Valley of the Kings. My family knew where it was worth while to dig. The secret knowledge was passed on from father to son, and my father used to take the treasures of the Pharaohs as if they were a part of his own inheritance. But one member of our family, my uncle Ali Gabri, thought differently. On a trip to Cairo he had met men who came from other countries and yet understood our language. They too wanted to dig, but not in order to gain wealth for themselves. And they were amazing men—they could even make stones speak. The walls of tombs and temples told them stories. Our people regarded them as unwanted intruders. But my uncle went over to their side, and when I was your age, he took me with him. Ever since then I have helped the excavators. . . . Megdi," Gurgar asked gently, and it struck the boy that this man whom he had never seen before should call him by name, "why are you, the son of an archaeologist, stabbing us in the back?"

Megdi's eyes flickered uneasily over the sand.

"Listen, my boy," Gurgar went on, "the people who lie buried below this ground were concerned above all that their names not be forgotten. Anyone who destroys any trace of them, as you have done, is disregarding their last will. Of course you could not know that," he softened the blow. "*We* have neglected to tell you, your father and I. I must speak to him this very day."

Megdi did not think well of this idea, and he made that quite clear.

Gurgar reassured him. "Your father will understand what you

19

have done better than anyone else." He looked searchingly at Megdi. "How old are you now—twelve?" he asked.

"Thirteen," Megdi replied. "What makes you think twelve?"

Gurgar's eyes sparkled. "Because your father was twelve when I pulled him out of a shaft."

Megdi sighed with relief.

"I have been working with archaeologists all my life, watching and helping them bring to life things long buried," Gurgar informed the boy. "I can tell you about their methods and—" he gripped the boy's arms with lean hands as dark and thin as the hands of a mummy—"and perhaps also about the things I experienced a few thousand years ago."

Megdi looked up at him. His gaze seemed to be coming out of unfathomable depths. But Megdi looked straight into his eyes and held his ground.

Gurgar winked. "I want something from you in return. There is one matter in which we old men cannot make any progress. Perhaps you can do something. Your father must take you along."

"Where?" Megdi asked in suspense.

"To the Valley of the Kings. You might equally well call it the Valley of the Excavators. Or of the robbers. I happen to know that your father will have business in western Thebes within a few days. We'll take you with us!"

"What am I to do there?"

"You will find out soon enough."

"And how about school?"

Gurgar raised his bushy eyebrows. "The school will have to manage without you for a change. I never wasted a day of my life going to school."

"You've never been to school? And you can read hieroglyphics!"

"I never quite forgot them," Gurgar said mysteriously. He glanced up at the sun. "Two hours after noon. We still have time. Let us go over to the Great Pyramid. In the shadow of that pyramid a discovery was made by men who knew their business. For two whole years they devoted all their ability and all their intelligence to the problem. They took the last fibre of wood, the last flake of gold leaf out of the shaft they had come upon. They brought out an enormous quantity of material, and still the shaft would not reveal its secret."

"How is that possible?"

"Come along," Gurgar said. "Up there, on the spot, I'll be better able to reconstruct the story for you."

A MYSTERIOUS FIND

The longer Megdi walked alongside the old man who had steered him from the path of grave robbing, the more certain he became that he had made a great discovery in the forbidden shaft: a discovery far more important than the little *ushabti* he held in his left hand, which did not speak to him. On the right walked an answerer who did not refuse to answer when he asked. Megdi felt glad that he was no longer alone. At the same time he was a little afraid that this strange man might vanish as suddenly as he had appeared.

In the hot sand their footsteps were almost inaudible. They passed the Sphinx. Before them the pyramids rose. The middle one appeared to be the tallest, and at the top there still clung some fragments of the stone sheath that had once covered all of it. The stone shimmered like snow in the sunlight. Gurgar went up to this, the Great Pyramid, also known as the pyramid of Cheops (the Greek name for the Pharaoh). Its eastern slope already lay in shadow, but the blocks of stone still felt warm underfoot as they climbed a few steps and sat down. Opposite them stood the tombs of the dignitaries and officials of Cheops' times—mighty benches of stone called mastabas, and three smaller pyramids which had been tombs for women of the royal house.

"It was over there!" Gurgar pointed to a spot on the wide road.

"But there isn't anything there," Megdi objected.

"That is how it seemed thirty years ago, too," Gurgar explained. "No one had ever noticed anything at that spot, although capable men had been working in this region since the turn of the century. But that is commonplace in excavation: year after year nothing extraordinary happens, and then everyone is amazed that something wonderful and incredible was not seen at once, after it has become obvious to all.

"The lucky finders were Americans who in 1902 had staked out an excavation area that included the Sphinx and the pyramids. They devoted thirty years to the task, and succeeded in exposing hundreds of graves, including the tombs of queens, princes, and princesses of the ruling family whom we now call the Fourth Dy-

Mastaba tombs of the Fourth Dynasty (section)

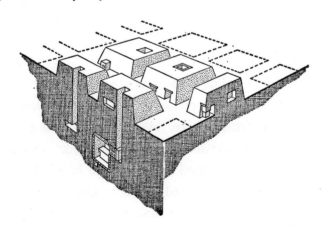

nasty. The most famous member of this dynasty was Pharaoh Cheops, the builder of this Great Pyramid.

"All the tombs were empty. They had been broken into thousands of years ago and robbed of their mummies and funeral gifts. Still, the archaeologists of the Egyptian expedition of Harvard and Boston Museum of Fine Arts, under the leadership of Dr. George Andrew Reisner, found many tomb paintings, reliefs, statues, and inscriptions. They even came across remains of foundation walls and of the black basalt sheathing of a temple to the dead which had once belonged to the Cheops pyramid. Yard by yard, sand, gravel, and building rubble were removed until roads with ancient pavement were revealed. And even this pavement was torn up so that it would be possible to see underneath the stone blocks. Early in December, 1924, the scientists came upon an incision in the rock. Their men dug deeper, and by December 12 their last doubts disappeared: they had discovered the base of a pyramid. To the north of this never-completed pyramid rose a ridge of rock. Alongside it they excavated a quarry where in Cheops' times stone blocks had been worked with the chisel. These were unexpected but not exactly world-shaking discoveries.

"But on the morning of February 9, 1925, while Reisner was back in America, lecturing, the expedition's photographer was having trouble taking pictures. He was an Egyptian named Abdu, and on this particular day his tripod would not stand straight; the ground was too hard and uneven. Abdu tried another spot, and one leg of his tripod broke through into a hole. Abdu examined the ground. It consisted neither of sand nor of loose gravel, but of plaster which had been used to fill a joint in the rock. He immedi-

24

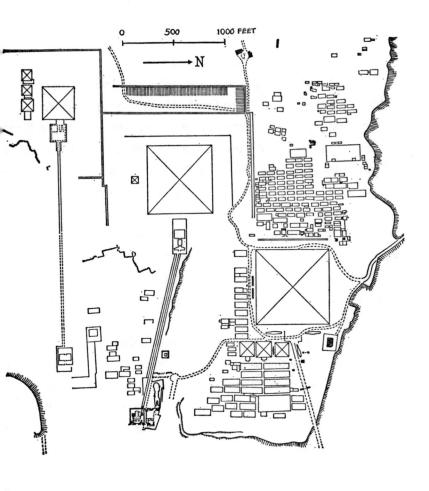

The pyramid area at Giza, with the pyramids of Cheops, Chephren and Mycerinus, the Great Sphinx (lower center), and mastabas

ately called over Reisner's assistant. With great care the men exposed an oval of plaster which proved to be a seal covering a rectangular incision. And this seal was uninjured—which meant that what lay below it had not been touched by anyone in the past.

"The first layer of barrier stones was removed, revealing a flight of stairs. By February 23, twelve steps had been cleared. The stairs led into a vertical shaft which had been filled with gravel and rubble and then closed off at the top by heavy blocks of stone. The top surfaces of these blocks were unhewn, to attempt to deceive any intruder into thinking he had come across natural rock. There was not the slightest trace of the superstructure which is usual in shaft graves. Layer by layer, the shaft was cleaned out. At a depth of thirty feet the archaeologists came across a tremendous slab of stone which had been inserted into the west wall of the shaft."

"Was that the door?" Megdi burst out eagerly.

"They assumed that it was, and worked to open it. But they found only a niche which contained the skull and three leg bones of an ox, two beer mugs, charcoal, and splinters of black basalt which undoubtedly had come from the flooring of the mortuary temple attached to the Great Pyramid. That was an important clue. What do you think it meant?"

"It meant that the shaft was dug after the temple was finished," Megdi replied.

"Good for you. Finished, or at least started. The workmen dug on, led by reis Achmed Said. The stone they cleared away was hauled to the surface by ropes and baskets. At a depth of forty feet were fragments of clay, and the walls showed dangerous cracks. Deeper down, parts of copper utensils turned up. But it was not un-

26

Chair of Queen Hetepheres

til the diggers reached a depth of eighty feet that they discovered a wall of stone blocks of the kind that were usually jointed together to close a tomb forever. On March 7, after thirteen laborious days, the first block was taken out. The glow of a candle fell into the chamber. Alan Rowe, one of Reisner's assistants, saw an alabaster sarcophagus and a confused heap of gilded rods and remains of household utensils from which the gold had flaked off in tiny scales. He could barely make out vases, jugs, and rings.

"As soon as the sun rose next morning, the discoverers descended into the shaft again. This time they had mirrors with which to reflect sunlight into the chamber. Individual objects could be made out more clearly. The gilded poles on the lid of the sarcophagus were unmistakably the supports of a collapsible canopy. The floor of the chamber was covered with flaked-off gold. There were lion paws from the legs of two chairs; the arms of the chairs had been bound in gold. The wood of chests and other furniture had rotted away, leaving only the gold bands that had bound it together or the gold sheathing that had covered it. There was jewellery; there

27

were vessels of clay and alabaster. Mats and baskets, jugs and dippers, were made of copper or gold. And when Rowe peered through binoculars at the wonderfully worked gold bands he found the name of a Pharaoh. The inscription read: Lord of the two crowns, Snefru. Snefru was the king who reigned over Egypt before Cheops and who during his reign completed three pyramids which now stand a day's journey from here to the south—in Dahshur and Medum."

"But then Snefru should have been buried in one of his pyramids there, instead of here," Megdi objected.

"That is just what puzzled the archaeologists," Gurgar said. "Why should the mightiest pyramid builder of all time be lying here? It was unthinkable. Besides, all the funerary gifts indicated that this was the tomb of a woman. Alabaster jugs bore such inscriptions as 'green eyeshade,' 'festive fragrance,' and 'finest Libyan ointment.' And there were anklets with thin plates of inlaid malachite set in lapis lazuli.

"Meanwhile Reisner had returned from the United States. He too thought many of the finds inexplicable. Among manicure sets, chests of clothes, and precious stuffs, were found copper chisels and other tools used for hewing tombs out of rock. What would these stonemasons' crude tools be doing among the household utensils of a woman to whom a Pharaoh had given funeral gifts? And what was the meaning of the bits of plaster and other rubble which had obviously been carried in from some other chamber? There were holes in the wall, rudely chiselled out and uncompleted. They had been hastily stuffed with stones and plastered so carelessly that the plaster still bore the fingerprints of the mason. Building materials lay about; in one of the chests there were alabaster chips from the sarcophagus."

"It sounds as if grave robbers broke in after all," Megdi said excitedly.

"No, Megdi, not robbers. Not at this tomb, anyway. These were all signs of haste, but there had certainly been no robbers, for wherever the diggers looked they saw gold, and other things of priceless value. The scientists went to work clearing the chamber with a thoroughness that had no example in the history of archaeology. This was the first unbroken tomb from that early period which is called the Old Kingdom. All the wood had been eaten away by dry rot, and much of it reduced to grey ash. The gold leaf had fallen away from it; eight layers of gold leaf lay one atop the other. Many of the fragments were so tiny they had to be taken up with pincers. The list of the bits and pieces covered seventeen hundred sheets of paper. Over a thousand photographs were taken of the exact positions of all such fragments before they were removed. Working with such care, the scientists were able to reconstruct a spacious canopy ten feet in height, two armchairs, a litter, and two chests—objects of such beauty that their match has not been found in any other tomb to the present day. Finally, on a shelf close to the floor,

Litter of Queen Hetepheres

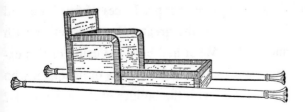

were found gold hieroglyphics, apparently from a chair that has disintegrated. These symbols spelled out the name of Hetepheres. Hetepheres was the wife of Snefru and the mother of Cheops. On December 16, 1926, the clearing of the chamber was completed, after 326 days of exacting work."

"But what about the sarcophagus?" Megdi demanded.

"I'm coming to that," Gurgar said, smiling at the boy's impatience. "On March 3, 1927, high Egyptian officials and noted archaeologists were invited by Reisner to attend the opening of the sarcophagus. Slowly, the heavy lid was raised a few inches—revealing an incredible sight. The sarcophagus was empty!

"Reisner was faced with a riddle. How could the sarcophagus have been robbed when the seal upon the entrance had been unbroken? There was no other shaft through which robbers might have entered. The walls of the shaft had not been touched. The sarcophagus could not have been broken open. Yet the scattered chips—and the fact that it was empty—indicated that something had happened.

"Where had the crime been committed? Reisner and his men investigated every detail all over again. Many little facts that they had neglected now acquired new meaning. For example, the plaster which could not have come from the chamber itself, the uncompleted walls of the chamber, and the masons' tools that had been left behind. The ceiling of the chamber was so low that it would have been impossible to set up the canopy. Pieces of furniture had been shoved into the chamber in the greatest haste, together with building materials and rubble. What had been the cause of this excessive haste, which was so ill suited to the dignity of a woman who had shared the throne of Egypt with the builder of three pyramids?

"After all the investigations were completed, Reisner proposed his explanation. Snefru's wife had died during the Pharaoh's lifetime. Presumably he had originally buried her near the pyramid which was to be his own dwelling place for eternity—in Dahshur. The smaller pyramid alongside his own had probably been the tomb for Hetepheres. After Snefru's death Cheops became king. He decided that his pyramid would be built at Giza, twelve miles further to the north. The burial city of Dahshur was therefore no longer directly under the eyes of the living Pharaoh. It may be that Cheops' overseers became negligent. Or else there was bribery. In any case, robbers had invaded the tomb of the queen mother, Hetepheres, at Dahshur. Probably the most precious funerary gifts were hidden in the wrappings of the mummy. The robbers snatched the mummy out of its sarcophagus, and took the inner coffin as well, which probably was of gold. Apparently they were disturbed by the guards and in fleeing with their booty, left a good many of the valuables behind. The crime was reported to the high priests of the burial city, who were responsible for the security of the graves. They were faced with an embarrassing situation; they had to confess to Cheops that the grave of his mother at Dahshur had been broken into. But apparently they did not dare to tell him the whole truth. For according to the beliefs of the Egyptians, destruction of a mummy meant that the dead person was dead for good and had been cheated of his chance for a life in the hereafter. They therefore said nothing about the empty coffin. Intent on saving his mother from the worst of all fates, Cheops ordered a second tomb prepared for her here in Giza in the vicinity of his own pyramid. In his anger at the unreliability of his men he may have insisted on setting a time limit for the work that was almost impossible to meet. Still, the persons responsible breathed easier. At the same time, their fear that the Pharaoh might ask to see his mother once more drove them to work at a frantic pace. As soon as the new tomb here at Giza had been crudely hewn out, everything the robbers had left behind at Dahshur was packed up. In the hustle, some of the plaster from the old tomb was stuffed into the boxes. The new chamber at Giza, which was much smaller than the old one at Dahshur, was stuffed full; then the shaft was filled in to the top and carefully sealed. So, you see, there was no robbery at this new tomb, only haste. The guardians of the tomb disguised the entrance so perfectly that it remained undiscovered for five thousand years. . . . Such, at any rate, was Reisner's explanation of the riddles," Gurgar concluded. "I have talked with my friend Achmed Said, foreman at this excavation, and he has told me how careful the archaeologists were to preserve the slightest clue."

"But what about the stolen mummy?" Megdi asked. "Were any signs of the robbery found in the small pyramid at Dahshur?"

"None whatsoever," Gurgar admitted.

"Then perhaps her grave was somewhere else."

"That is possible," Gurgar agreed. "You see, there are still questions that need looking into."

"Is anything known about the queen's life?"

"Hardly anything."

"And about her son, Cheops?"

"Not much more, in spite of his fame," Gurgar said. "There is nothing left of him except a statuette as tiny as your hand."

Opposite: *Pyramids and Great Sphinx at Giza* (above); *Shore of the Nile at Aswân* (below)

"*And* the pyramids!" Megdi added emphatically.

"Yes, those will not quite fit into the palm of your hand," Gurgar said. He studied the shadow cast by the pyramid. "Only half past three," he declared. Glancing at his wrist watch, Megdi saw that Gurgar's estimate was exactly right. There was plenty of time; Megdi's father usually stayed at the funerary ship until five o'clock.

"Have you been in the cave yet?" Gurgar asked suddenly. "In the lowest chamber of the Great Pyramid? There is something there that I wonder about continually. In the oldest history of the pyramid an island is mentioned, an island of the Nile which is supposed to be exactly under its apex."

"But surely enough people have already looked for that."

"Not our kind of people," Gurgar said a little condescendingly. "Come, let us pay a visit to the cave. We have a good hour yet."

Light-footedly, he descended the steps, with Megdi at his side. Tourists from many nations approached them down the broad road. Many of them looked back at the boy who seemed rich enough to afford a dragoman all his own.

Abruptly, Gurgar turned in another direction. "Just a short detour," he explained. "I want to show you the place where I lived for two years—together with a man from England and my uncle, Ali Gabri."

Gurgar led Megdi to a nearby cliff which, like the entire area, was strewn with burial vaults. One of these, larger than the rest, but cut into the solid rock, had a door and two windows. "The Englishman took this for headquarters," Gurgar explained. "And here lived my uncle, a Negro boy, and myself."

Opposite: *Dignitary of the Old Kingdom with writing utensils*

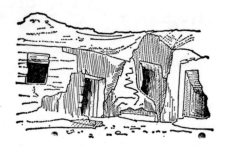

*Tombs in Giza which served
Petrie as dwellings*

Megdi glanced into the old burial places. They were empty now, stark cells entirely of stone. "Two years?" Megdi asked. "You didn't mind it?"

"Not a bit. We thought the vaults made pleasant and comfortable quarters," Gurgar said. "Ali Gabri had come here earlier with other investigators of the pyramids. He knew every nook and corner in this vicinity. And Sir Flinders Petrie—that was the Englishman's name—felt at home between these walls which, as he said, were built for eternity. They were cool in the summer, warm in winter. Petrie had brought all sorts of measuring tools with him. By day he and Ali Gabri circled around the pyramid taking measurements. At twilight, dressed only in a pair of shorts, he would vanish into the corridors and passages of the pyramid. At midnight he would reappear, go back to his rocky cell, and sit calculating and writing."

"What was he trying to do?" Megdi asked.

"Track down the builders of the pyramids," Gurgar said. "Like us."

IN SEARCH OF CHEOPS

They returned to the broad highway, traversed the square which lies along the northern flank of the Great Pyramid, and ascended the steps to the entrance, which lies at a height of some fifty feet. Gurgar exchanged a few words with the gaffer who stood by the door, and was handed two keys. Then he beckoned Megdi to follow him, and started off into the narrow corridor which, slanted downward. Megdi knew this corridor; it led to Cheops' chamber and the so-called Queen's Chamber. After some seventy feet the corridor forked, the branch open to the public leading upward again. Gurgar, however, unlocked an iron gate, switched on his flashlight, and made his way carefully along a passage that led still farther downward. Megdi followed close behind him.

"This shaft descends for somewhat over three hundred feet," Gurgar said. "Afterwards we go a short way on the level, and then we are there."

The floor and walls were slippery, sweating under the weight of the two and one-half million blocks of stone above them. The descent was difficult. Suddenly Gurgar disappeared. Megdi found him standing in an opening in the wall. The old man pointed upward. "This shaft is called the well—although it was never used as a well."

"What was it used for then?"

"You will see on your way out." Gurgar went on along the original passage. Another few steps, and a dim cavern opened before them. It was about ten feet high, twenty feet wide, and more than twice as long.

Megdi thought the name "cave" suited it well, for it was a weird place, with rough, unfinished walls. In the farther wall a tunnel began. Megdi flashed his light into it; there was nothing there except rock. He let the cone of light glide along the floor. Shadows stirred on floor and walls.

"There's a hole! Did the archaeologists or robbers make it?" Megdi exclaimed.

Gurgar shook his head. "This hole remains a problem for me. Undoubtedly it is older than any of the intruders. It was created when the pyramid was not much higher than a house. At that time Cheops abandoned the original building plan. He did not change the outward appearance of the pyramid, but he decided to move the burial chamber to the pyramid's centre of gravity. That made new passages necessary. Later Cheops changed his plan a second time. He had the Great Hall and the ultimate Royal Chamber made. The sarcophagus was let down from above, and only then were the granite walls of the chamber built up around it, layer by layer. The roof was made of fifty-six blocks, each of which weighed fifty-four tons. Those blocks were cut from the rock at Aswân, brought more than 450 miles down the Nile, and like all the other blocks, were

36

dragged from the dock to the pyramid up an enormous ramp. Hard work, but the men who did it sang as they toiled. Every block, they thought, was making a contribution not only to their Pharaoh's immortality, but also to their own."

The old man sat down on the edge of the opening in the ground and drew Megdi over to his side. "It is a hole like so many others —but perhaps also it is testimony that there is a kernel of truth in the story of the Nile island under the pyramid."

"But the Nile is far away," Megdi objected.

"History speaks of an underground canal. This hole suggests that a shaft to a greater depth was planned," Gurgar pointed out. "Of course, 'island in the Nile' was meant rather poetically. The Greek historian Herodotus heard of such a supposed island under the Great Pyramid when he visited Egypt twenty-five hundred years ago. There were dragomans even then, and they told foreigners who wanted to see the greatest of the Seven Wonders of the World the stories they had heard from their fathers. The Pharaoh for whom the pyramid was built, so they said, had been a tyrant, a flouter of the gods, an oppressor of his subjects. For twenty years he imposed forced labour upon his people. A hidden canal was to bring the Nile's water of life up to the pyramid, making an island deep in the rock upon which the sarcophagus was to be placed. And above this a mountain of two and a half million blocks of stone would be erected, solely in order for the Pharaoh to have a secure hiding place for eternity. There his body and his enormous treasures would rest. The tyrant exacted the lives of a hundred thousand men every year, and left strict orders that the pyramid was to be closed from inside, even though it meant that the work-

37

men given this task were buried alive. But retribution was not long in coming. Soon after his death grave robbers made a pauper of the cruel Pharaoh. Worse still, they burned his mummy, thus removing him entirely from this and the next world.

"That was the story the dragomans told. Herodotus took the tale at its face value. But there were others who credited only half of it. They were hungry for treasure and they doubted that the Pharaoh's riches had already been stolen from him, for nowhere in the pyramid were there any traces of robbery.

"The first man to open the pyramid publicly was Caliph al-Mamun, the son of Harun al-Rashid, caliph of the Arabian Nights. At al-Mamun's orders, a team of architects and workmen set about breaking into the pyramid in A.D. 820. In the middle of the northern wall, at the level of the thirteenth layer of blocks, they began their borings. Day after day, week after week, month after month, they attacked the great blocks of stone. Two smiths were kept constantly at work sharpening chisels—until it became clear that chisels were too feeble. Then the caliph had the blocks of stone heated with fires, and had cold vinegar poured over them until they cracked. But still no corridor or chamber appeared. The pyramid remained stubbornly solid. When a shaft over a hundred feet long had been driven into the stone, the workmen nearly mutinied. Then the pyramid itself suddenly spoke. Inside it, close to the end of the shaft, a stone fell. The men were able to gauge the direction of the sound. Now the masons worked on with redoubled zeal, and at last they pierced through into a corridor that slanted upward. They squeezed into it and followed it back to the hidden entrance which had not been opened for thousands of years. They

38

found a block which served as a secret door, and lifted it right out of its hinges, into which it had been set so that it could revolve. The entrance was at the level of the eighteenth layer, twenty-five feet east of the centre. This placing it off centre was the first of the many deceptions with which the pyramid builders had attempted to mislead robbers.

"Penetrating farther into the interior, the caliph's workmen encountered granite blocks that resisted all their chisels. They worked their way around these through softer stone and reached a passage that forked. One branch led horizontally to an empty chamber. The treasure-hunters did not know that now they were directly under the apex of the pyramid. Disappointed, they examined the naked stone walls, chiselled a few holes into a niche they discovered in the eastern side of the chamber, and finally abandoned the place. They were likewise disappointed by the hall higher up. This was a high, narrow room roofed over by seven overlapping layers of stone, and their bitterness reached its peak when, having worked their way through an antechamber into the granite tomb in which the sarcophagus stood, they found it broken open, robbed. So much toil and no reward! In vain they knocked holes in the walls, tore up parts of the floor. Cheops' chamber had neither secrets nor treasures to yield. Hope flickered once more when they discovered a narrow shaft immediately behind the blocks of granite which they had circuited. This was the 'well' which ended in this 'cave.' It, too, offered no treasures. The pyramid had rejected the caliph. He returned to Baghdad, and died soon afterwards. The Arabs were left with a horror of the pyramids which remained with them almost to the present.

"A thousand years passed. From across the sea came an emperor named Napoleon. He defeated the Mamelukes who then ruled Egypt. While his generals were climbing the pyramid, the emperor amused himself by calculating that in the three pyramids before him there was enough stone to build a wall ten feet high around all of France. The stones in the Great Pyramid alone, cut into blocks a foot square and laid end to end, would go around the world at the Equator.

"With Napoleon a new age began for ancient Egypt. The men who pierced the pyramid now were no longer seeking treasures. They wanted to solve the mysteries that Cheops had built into his pyramid. Before long they had established the external measurements. The tallest of these towering solid triangles, which rose up like giant staircases against the sky (the Egyptians had called them Akhet Khufu, 'Horizon of Cheops'), had risen to a height of 482 feet before the loss of its apex and stone mantle. It was still 450 feet high. The base lines on each side measured about 750 feet and were aligned exactly north, south, east, and west.

"The interior still remained to be explored. A British consul named Davison, unable to believe that in this whole vast structure there should be only the three chambers discovered up till then, hit upon the idea of asking the pyramid itself for guidance. He stood in the King's Chamber and shouted. The pyramid replied. There came an echo from above. So there must be a hollow space up there. Davison sent for a ladder and a group of workmen for the purpose of breaking an opening through the top of the front wall of the gallery. He himself was the first to climb the ladder and to see that the opening he had deduced already existed. He crawled into a low chamber about twenty feet long. It was quite empty.

"Forty years later an English colonel discovered four more chambers by driving a vertical shaft up from Davison's room. These four additional chambers were also empty. But in one of them the colonel found the name *Khufu,* the Egyptian word for Cheops. Upon closer study the purpose of the chambers was discovered. They served to relieve the pressure on the King's Chamber, so that it would not be crushed by the enormous weight of the stone above and around it. Calculation showed that one chamber would have been sufficient, but the ancients decided in favour of fivefold safety.

"In 1872 an engineer named Dickson made a further discovery. He found two narrow air shafts leading diagonally upward from the middle chamber, which had been erroneously called the 'Queen's Chamber.' Similar air shafts led to the King's Chamber. What had they been for? To bring fresh air to the Pharaoh's mummy? There were all sorts of explanations. Some saw in the pyramid a monument to a tyrant, or a hiding place for treasures; others thought it an astronomical observatory, or even the very granary in which Joseph had hoarded grain for the seven lean years. And finally there were some who imagined that they could read the course of world history to the end of time from the numerical relationships. One of these people was caught by Petrie secretly filing at one of the blocks of granite so that it would fit his calculations . . . Petrie, the 'crazy Englishman' I worked for, who set up headquarters for two years in a tomb, would have no part of any such wild theories. All he cared to do was to measure the pyramid. Others had measured it before him, and everyone had come out with a different result. Petrie was interested in precise measurements.

"Petrie once explained to me and the Negro boy the world of

difference there is between one kind of precision and another kind. The precision with which a gardener lays out his flower beds would not do in building a house. And a bridge has to be constructed with even greater precision, or it will collapse. Even the precision of the bridge builder is not enough for the lenses of a telescope. Petrie had instruments he could rely on, he had the necessary patience, and he had the courage to crawl into corridors into which no Arab except Ali Gabri and me were willing to follow him. Several times he barely escaped being entombed inside a pyramid. But after two years of painstaking labour he had solved the problem he had set himself. His work had revealed the true miracle of the Great Pyramid. For it was an astounding structure which those ancient builders had set down in the midst of the desert, astounding in terms of its precision. To give only one example of the extraordinary workmanship of those builders: the limestone mantle of the pyramid was composed of blocks of stone set so close together that not even a sheet of paper could be inserted between them. It was the same

Longitudinal north-south section through the Cheops Pyramid

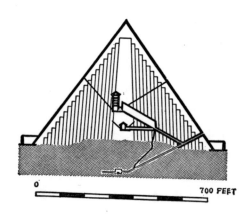

0   700 FEET

with the granite slabs that lined the walls of the inner chambers."

The old man's eyes sparkled with excitement as he described this. Then he noticed the unspoken question on Megdi's face.

"I felt as you do," the old man said. "I was just about your age at the time, and at first I was disappointed. What had the Englishman found out, after all? Nothing but figures. That was my first thought. But after a while I realized that Petrie had learned more from the stones than Herodotus had from the dragomans. He had learned what kind of man had built this pyramid. The layout of the passages told a story. The Pharaoh who had built the Great Pyramid was not a man inclined to flout the gods."

Megdi looked up at Gurgar with undisguised doubt.

"Come along," the old man said. "See for yourself!" He stood up and went back along the corridor to the point where it began to slope. There Gurgar pointed up. Then he switched off his flashlight. Far, far above, caught in the long tube of the air shaft, a tiny patch of sky glimmered, and in its stone-framed orifice there appeared, although it was broad daylight outside, a single star.

"The star that remains unwearyingly in the sky: the North Star," Gurgar whispered. "The shaft is so placed that it points directly to this star. The Egyptians considered the North Star the handle of the sacred implement with which the gods touched the mouths of the dead to resurrect them for the afterlife. In no other pyramid is this passageway aimed with such accuracy at the centre of the firmament."

Megdi looked thoughtfully up at the star which twinkled high above. Gurgar went on with rising enthusiasm: "There is another ancient story about Cheops, a story even older than Herodotus'

43

tale, but current in this region up to recent times. The story kept alive the reputation of Cheops as a heartless tyrant. It seems that in the days of the Pharaoh there had been a magician named Dedi who was said to be able to replace a severed head upon its body. Cheops sent for the wonder-worker and wanted him to demonstrate his magic on a criminal who had been condemned to death. The magician objected, and asked instead for a goose to be decapitated. This was done. Dedi put the head in one corner of the room, the lifeless body in the opposite corner, said his spell, and the headless goose waddled toward its head, slipped it on its neck, and began to cackle like any normal goose. The same was done with a cow. The Pharaoh then declared himself content. The story is told to illustrate the inhuman qualities of Cheops, but we can see in it quite another meaning. For when the magician demurred at using a man for such an experiment, did not the Pharaoh see what was meant, that no man, even a condemned criminal, could be treated as a beast? No, the tale portrays Cheops as far from a monster, in fact as a man of great moderation."

Gurgar switched on his flashlight again, took the boy by the arm, and drew him into the fork in the passage. "You first," he said.

It was necessary to climb up this passage, but the slope was far from being as steep as the one into which Megdi had entered by himself earlier that afternoon. The "well" was comfortably wide and offered plenty of footholds. Slowly they made their way through living rock and then, the last ten or fifteen yards, through a passage between hewn stone blocks. At last there was another gate before them. Megdi opened it with the key that Gurgar handed o him. They came out precisely at the spot where the sloping Great Hall and the horizontal passage to the "Queen's Chamber" began—and to the corridor that led to the outside. Gurgar pointed to the granite blocks with which this corridor had been sealed from within, sealed so thoroughly that the caliph's men had been forced to chisel around them. "This is the important spot," Gurgar declared. "Only after the dead Pharaoh had been laid in his sarcophagus and the funeral party had left the pyramid, were these granite blocks put in from the inside to seal the passage. Once this was done, the workmen who had carried out this final task inside the pyramid could no longer escape through the shaft."

"But there was still the well," Megdi objected.

"Bravo," Gurgar exclaimed with pleasure. "You have seen through the myth about the cruel tyrant."

Carefully he closed the iron door behind him. "How late is it?" he asked. "Without the sun, I am in the dark as far as time is concerned."

Megdi flashed his light upon his wrist watch. "Already past five!" he noted in alarm.

The two of them hurried out of the pyramid. Gurgar returned the keys to the gaffer. The square in front of the pyramid was still crowded with tourists, camel drivers and dragomans. Megdi caught sight of his father walking towards the Mena House, where the tram for Cairo started.

"You may as well start preparing," Gurgar said, "for joining our expedition. Ask your father to show you how to write the name of Cheops in hieroglyphics. Or that of Hetepheres. It's about time you

45

started learning hieroglyphics. You should be able to read at least few royal names by the time we go to the Valley of the King And now run along; run, run, you still have time to catch him!"

In thirteen leaps Megdi was down the thirteen steps. By the time he reached the terminal, his father was already seated in the tram. "I nearly missed you," Megdi said breathlessly.

He did not mention Gurgar.

DECIPHERER OF THE
HIEROGLYPHICS

He caught me at it, too," Megdi's father confessed, when Megdi
t last told the story of his adventure. "Oh, he's a great old fel-
ow. Always on the lookout for future archaeologists. It bothers
im, I think, that visitors from all the countries in the world come
o the land of the Pharaohs, while we Egyptians for the most part
o not concern ourselves with our great traditions."

"Is it true that you are going to Thebes soon?" Megdi probed.

"For a few days," Father replied.

"Gurgar said you ought to take me along. He said he thought I
would be useful."

Father laughed. "I know what he has in mind—the idea is one
f his obsessions."

"Is it a good idea?"

"I hope that he can put it across. You see, there's an old village
ear the Valley of the Kings. Its name is Qurna. Many of the in-
abitants do not live in houses, but in tombs of the time of the
Pharaohs. As you can imagine, the living conditions are not very
ood in such places. Now the government is building a whole new
illage for the people, a mile away from the old one. But the
Qurnese don't want to leave their hovels."

"Why not?"

"Because as long as they stay there they will ransack the tomb for what they can find—although it is illegal."

"But why does Gurgar want me to go there with you?"

"We can't do anything in that region until we've dislodged the inhabitants. The older people are dead set against leaving. Gurgar wants to appeal to the younger people. But he thinks it would be better if a boy were to talk with them."

"Then may I really come?"

"If Gurgar thinks you will be useful," Father said, "I'm willing. Sometimes he knows more about these things than I do. I imagine your teachers will excuse you. How are you doing in school at the moment?"

"Could be worse," Megdi said.

"Much would depend on how you approached the Qurnese," Father went on, his enthusiasm mounting as he spoke. "If you could only make one or two boys of the village see what is at stake . . . All they care about is selling their finds on the black market. They are just grave robbers, of the most old-fashioned sort. But they are doing great harm to future research."

Megdi pricked up his ears at the phrase "future research."

"Gurgar says," he hinted, "that I ought to be able to read at least the names of the most important kings in hieroglyphics."

"Ask him to teach you then," Father said mischievously.

"But he's not a trained archaeologist like you. He can't really read hieroglyphics, can he?"

Opposite: *King Zoser's Step Pyramid and the White Walls in Saqqara* (above); *Head of a statue of Chephren* (below)

"Didn't he tell you that he knew them from memory?"

"Yes, he did, but that can't mean . . ." Megdi said a bit uncertainly.

"Gurgar knows a great deal," Father said. He sounded in earnest now. "You can learn a lot from him. I've learned a lot myself from Gurgar."

"But couldn't you teach me about hieroglyphics?"

"You are peskier than a swarm of mosquitoes," Father groaned. But he seemed quite good-natured as he brought down from one of the book-shelves a thick book, and leafed through its pages. He stopped at an illustration. It was, Megdi saw as he pressed close to the book, the picture of a stone slab. The stone was covered with script. The top part was in hieroglyphics.

"It all began with this stone," Father declared. "You see, there are three kinds of script on it. The upper two scripts were complete mysteries. But the lower section is made up of Greek letters. Some day you will learn them in school. And it was by grace of that section in Greek that the Egyptian script was finally deciphered."

"Who did decipher it? An Egyptian?"

"No, it was a Frenchman, but a man who seemed born to bring to life the mysteries of ancient Egypt. From the time he was a boy he was intrigued by things Egyptian, and most of all by the enigma of the hieroglyphics. He drew the queer little pictures on the margins of his schoolbooks, and carved them into the wood of his desk. From the time he was your age he had firmly made up his mind that he was going to be the one to solve the mystery of Egyptian picture writing."

Opposite: *Man with sacrificial ox; tomb of Ptahhotep in Saqqara*

"What was his name?" Megdi asked, feeling a bit envious of this boy who had done something so noteworthy—the sort of thing Megdi would like to do himself.

"Champollion," his father said. "Jean François Champollion."

"Did he live a long time ago?"

"He was born in 1790," Father answered. "Yes, that was quite a while ago."

"Did he come to Egypt?" Megdi asked. "Is that how he saw the hieroglyphics?"

"No," Father replied. "He saw them while still in France. Later in life, to be sure, he did come to Egypt. But by that time he had steeped himself in Egyptian studies. He had even hit upon the clue for reading the Rosetta stone."

"You mean this stone in the picture?" Megdi asked, pointing to the illustration in the book.

"That's right," Father said. "It was discovered by a soldier of Napoleon's—you've already learned in your history class how Napoleon set out to conquer Egypt. The French were wonder-struck by all the relics of a great ancient civilization, and they shipped an enormous amount of loot back to France, not really knowing what most of it represented, for they could not yet read the picture writing. One day a soldier discovered a tablet of black granite, large as a table top, covered with writing. He found it at the village of Rosetta, near the mouth of the western arm of the Nile, where the French were building fortifications. The soldier called the attention of his officer, Lieutenant Boussard, to the inscribed signs, and Boussard found that he was able to read the lower third of the stone, for the writing was Greek. Scholars applied themselves to the problem of deciphering the upper sections, for here, they sensed, was something of a clue. The Greek text was obviously a translation of the Egyptian. But try as they might, they could not make sense of the little figures. At last Champollion found the key with which to unlock the mysteries of the Rosetta stone. An obelisk had been found which likewise had texts in Greek and in hieroglyphics. In both cases, the Greek texts contained two royal names: Ptolemy and Cleopatra. And in both cases the corresponding hieroglyphic texts contained two symbols which were distinguished from the other signs by being circled with a sort of elongated ring, which nowadays we call a cartouche. Champollion experimented with the theory that these two 'special' signs might be royal names, the name of Cleopatra and the name of Ptolemy. He tried it out, and suddenly the words began to fall into place. The symbols were no longer inexplicable. Moreover, he discovered what nobody had thought possible: that the hieroglyphics were alphabetic scripts which had developed out of picture writing. It became evident to him that the same word could be written two different ways in hieroglyphics: with a single picture, or by the use of several pictorial signs. For example, you could write the word 'face' simply by drawing a face. Or else you could spell it out with letters making up the word for 'face.' But even the single character could be misleading. It was necessary to bring an enormous amount of psychological acuteness to the reading of the picture writing. For

51

example, the hieroglyphic showing a scorpion in a palace with a falcon sitting on the palace wall did not mean, 'Falcon fighting with scorpion for palace,' but rather, 'King Scorpion.' The falcon showed that the Pharaoh named Scorpion was at the same time the god whom the ancient Egyptians conceived in the guise of a falcon.

"Or take another example of the trickiness of hieroglyphics. There is an inscription on a stone palette such as the Egyptians used for grinding face paint. It shows two giraffes and a date palm. Before Champollion discovered the underlying principles of hieroglyphics, scholars would have read such a message: 'Giraffes in an oasis.' This was all very well, but did not seem to lead to anything. Champollion understood that the giraffes and date palm represented some ceremonial wish. The ancient Egyptians were using these signs in a figurative sense. Giraffes with their long necks were taken by the Egyptians as good and vivid signs for the concept of 'foreseeing.' Date palms, which yield both shade and fruit, were taken as representations of 'pleasant peacetime.' A picture showing giraffes grazing beneath date palms meant: 'Looking forward to a pleasant time of peace.'

"To take the pictures literally, you see, was to be bogged down instantly in a host of disconnected ideas. What Champollion did was to track down the same symbol again and again, until by many comparisons the right meaning could be deduced. He also discovered that in later writing the Egyptians made use of explanatory signs which helped to clarify the symbols. There were even two kinds of writing, a so-called priestly script, the hieratic; and a people's script, the demotic. You might call these shorthand hieroglyphics. They were easier to read and write than the traditional characters. For a literate Egyptian all three forms were easily readable. But European scholars had been hopelessly at a disadvantage, for they could not have the slightest conception of the Egyptian way of thought until the writing had been interpreted.

"Champollion had spent more than fourteen years struggling with the ancient Egyptian script by the time he at last set foot in Egypt. He was the leader of a small band of scholars who came to see the temples and the tombs, the wall paintings, the sculptures, and the rolls of papyrus left by a civilization which had done its best to win eternity. Thanks to them, the kingdom of the Pharaohs was to have an afterlife. Champollion himself has described vividly the excitement with which he and his companions looked at the monuments that rose out of the desert in Thebes and in the Valley of the Kings.

"Back in France, only a year and a half of life and work were left to Champollion. While still a student, he had ventured the opinion that Egypt had to be explained by the Egyptians. Certainly no other European had shown such an uncanny insight into the mystery of hieroglyphics. For quite a while there were specialists who opposed his interpretation of hieroglyphics. But as time went on, more and more scholars began to see that only Champollion had provided a fruitful method. Scholars of many nations helped to complete what he had begun. For work of that sort, like all archaeological work, Megdi, depends upon many, many people labouring for many, many years."

Megdi stared rather crestfallen at his toes.

"Does that discourage you?" Father asked. "It should not. Some-

53

times a genius comes along, like Champollion, who opens doors for others. Sometimes this type of genius manifests itself in a young person. One such young genius was Heinrich Brugsch. He was a boy your age when he became fascinated by the Egyptian collection in the Berlin museum. Since children were not allowed into the collection unless an adult accompanied them, the boy took to slipping in by stealth. The old museum attendant caught him copying the mysterious signs carved into many of the stones. The old man and the boy became friends, and young Brugsch was able to visit the museum as often as he liked. Word of this extraordinary boy reached the museum director. Here was an interest worth cultivating, the director thought, and he invited young Brugsch to his own house, which was a treasure-trove of Egyptian objects. The boy studied them. He was still a student at the *Gymnasium* when he drew up a grammar of the Egyptian demotic script.

"Brugsch, too, finally realized the goal of his dreams and went to Egypt. He lived on the simple foods of the poorest natives—on lentils, beans, onions—and lodged in old vaults and temples. He seemed indifferent to the hardships of his life, to the snakes and scorpions that infested his quarters, or to the meagreness of his diet. It was enough for him that he could study the monuments at close hand.

"Gurgar has told you, hasn't he, of the English archaeologist for whom he worked, who also lived in an ancient burial vault? This was Flinders Petrie, and you will hear of him often, for he did more than any other man to reconstruct the history of the Pharaohs. He spent seventy years of his life at the task, having begun his training as an archaeologist when he was only a boy. His father

Cylinder seal of the Middle Kingdom, with inscription rolled out

had been an amateur student of antiquity, and had taught the boy the techniques of surveying, which were later to stand him in good stead. It was Petrie's father, too, who originated the principle that the earth must be sifted as carefully in excavations as in prospecting for gold. By the age of ten the young Petrie had mastered Latin, Greek, and French. He was just twelve when he heard of an excavation on the Isle of Wight. The remains of a Roman country house were being dug up. But he was horrified at the carelessness and haste with which the work was being conducted. The soil should be taken away inch by inch, literally scraped away, he declared, so that even the most insignificant-looking shards remained in their place.

"This tenet, which he insisted on from the first, was to be the guiding motive of his work, right up to the time of his death in 1942. He was the world's greatest authority on shards, and could unlock a thousand secrets with them. By means of those he had collected in Abydos he succeeded in identifying the names of nineteen kings of the early period. All at once, light was cast upon four centuries of early Egyptian history which had previously been ut-

55

terly dark. Now historians began to have some inkling of how the Old Kingdom had come into being, and how it was that the pyramids had risen out of the desert."

Father closed the big book. "Enough for one lecture," he said. "The day after tomorrow we shall look at a few things, for I have business in Saqqara. That is where the earliest of the pyramids stands, the Zoser pyramid."

THE WHITE WALLS

The sun had not yet risen above the horizon when Megdi and his father set out in their car for Saqqara. The distance was only some twelve miles, but the road along the canal was rough, and the car bumped so that Megdi was soon wide awake and fully conscious of the treat that this was going to be. The flat fields of the Nile basin were not clearly visible in the early morning light. They had been driving about fifteen minutes when Megdi made out the pyramids of Abusir on their right, modest mounds compared to the stone giants of Giza. Shortly afterwards another pyramid came into view, one that rose in graduated planes like six giant steps. The road curved toward the low plateau which formed the pedestal for the step pyramid. The wheels of the car began to grind in the sand. They stopped in front of the house which Auguste Mariette, the lucky excavator, had built upon the site of the most tremendous archaeological field in Egypt, so that he would not have to waste time going back and forth. It was still some distance to the Zoser pyramid, and Megdi wondered why they were not driving on. Father said that they had better walk some of the way, to warm up.

They walked across the sand toward the pyramid. The air and the seemingly endless desert were of the same silvery grey. Megdi tried to locate the horizon beyond the pyramid. He could not decide for certain where the desert stopped and the sky began. When he looked back, however, the horizon was perfectly clear. In the east the cliffs rose sharply, almost blackly silhouetted against the rays of the rising sun.

As father and son stood there, the whole panorama of the past seemed to unfold before them.

In the earliest days the kings were entombed in simple houses, or burial mounds. But in the Third Dynasty something new and wonderful happened: an architect named Imhotep erected six hills one upon another, the Sun throne to which the six vast steps which Megdi had just seen, led. Here the Pharaoh would be laid after his death. This was the first pyramid, and it was constructed out of stone blocks. During his lifetime, Zoser had lived in a palace made of perishable mud bricks, wood, and reed mats. But the eternal residence which Imhotep built for him could withstand the sands of the desert and the waters of the Nile. It was as imperishable as the soul of the Pharaoh.

The ancient Egyptians built their houses often of bricks made from the mud of the Nile. Traces of the oldest settlements can still be found on heights along the river and on the fringes of the delta. People settled in those areas where tracks on firm ground indicated the presence of game, for the first inhabitants of the Nile district lived by hunting. Originally the sea extended deep into this land, and the river banks were marshlands, given over to the crocodiles nd hippopotamuses. But in the course of thousands of years the Nile won more and more of the delta away from the sea. Year after year the river laid down *kemi,* the black soil upon which things grow. Rainfall was heavy then and the great plain was a paradise for lions and bison, for the wild ass, antelope, ostrich, giraffe, elephant, hedgehog, and rabbit. But as the climate changed and the rains grew sparser, the grazing grounds turned to sand. Much of the game departed, and the hunters were lured closer to the Nile. Now they depended upon birds and fish, water buffalo, and hippopotamus. They built round huts which they entered through a hole in the roof, climbing down steps made of the thighbones of hippos. They fabricated nets and lines for fishing. As time passed they became more and more successful in developing the surrounding swamp into tillable fields. The hunters now became breeders of domestic animals, tillers of the soil, and sailors.

Pictures on rock walls and on thousands of clay vessels show the way they built their boats, first out of bundles of reeds, then out of

Donkeys threshing (Old Kingdom)

wood. Graves, too, record this transformation; the earliest one ha[s] caches of dogs and hunting weapons; the later ones provided sma[ll] boats, without sails for the journey downstream, and with sails if th[e] deceased must travel south. As for the living, they had need to b[e] industrious in their new life pattern. Wells were dug and fields lai[d] out; barley, wheat, beans, leeks, and onions were planted for food[,] flax for fabric. The farmers used wooden ploughs, hoes, and sick[-] les. Donkeys helped to bring in the harvest and trample the grai[n] on the threshing floor. Cattle and sheep, pigs, goats, and pigeon[s] were raised; ducks, geese, and cranes tamed and fattened. In th[e] treeless land, palms and tamarisks, figs and pomegranate trees[,] sycamores and grapevines were planted.

The Nile completely dominated the lives of the ancient Egyp[-] tians. They called South "upstream" and spoke of their land a[s] "the two banks," even using the term "Nile from Heaven" for rain[.] Then as now, the Nile made the three seasons of Egypt: Flood[,] Sowing, and Harvest. Two-thirds of the year the Nile flows lik[e] other rivers, its waters reflecting the blue of the sky, the yellow o[f] the desert, and the green of the fields. But in the summer the Nil[e] bursts forth raging and red as blood between Krofi and Mofi, the[,] pillars of the granite gate near Aswân, and in October it reaches it[s] highest level.

In bygone days, famine or abundance depended upon how high[,] the Nile rose. If only twenty feet, she would not enrich enough o[f] the adjacent land, and crops would be sparse. If she rose thirty feet[,] she swept away the dams and houses which the people had built a[s] near to the river as they dared. Hapi, the God of the Nile, was a[,] two-faced god. He brought prosperity and disaster.

The Nile's flooding of Egypt year after year forced the mutually hostile tribes along its route to take up tools instead of weapons and to unite their labour in order to build canals and dikes. The more tribes that joined together, the more easily the Nile was tamed. The life of the peasant became more secure as the years passed, although it was a life of endless toil and scant daily rations of three loaves of bread and two jugs of beer. Finally rulers of the Oldest Land, around This, succeeded in uniting North and South.

King Menes, the Victor, built his capital at the spot where Upper and Lower Egypt met. It was called the White Walls, and later Memphis. Menes is said to be the first Pharaoh who wore both crowns, the shallow red crown of the delta country and the high white crown of the South. His work of unification remained so memorable an act in the eyes of the Egyptians that every future ruler symbolically repeated it when he ascended the throne. To immortalize the union, the Pharaoh was called "Lord of the two Lands," "Wearer of both Crowns." His capital city was called the "Balance of the two Lands," and two royal tombs were prepared for him, one in the North and one in the South. High above all common humanity, the Pharaoh sat enthroned like the sun above the earth. He was responsible for the task of guiding the Nile so that it would bring life, not death. He had to see to it that the desert did not reach to the Nile, but the Nile to the desert. That was his function—one worthy of a god. Therefore he was looked upon as a god on earth, his palace being designated as the "horizon," his royal barge as the "star of both lands." He himself was also the Great House—the heaven from which came all benefits for his people. The ancient Egyptians regarded their Pharaoh as a being descended from a higher world, just like the gods who had governed the earth before him.

In the most ancient times, so the people believed, the Sun had been king of the lands of the Nile. And even before that?

Before Heaven had yet arisen,
Before man had yet arisen,
Before even the gods were,
And before even death was,
There was One who appeared upon his throne,
As his heart instructed him, and glowed mightily in the beginning,
And the world lay in silence before his greatness.
And he spoke the word into the silence,
And opened the eyes of the beings which he created,
Let each of them know the way that was laid down for it,
And made their hearts so, that they could see him.

Ptah, the Creator, awakened the world by his word. He created the gods as his assistants. First he created Khnemu, the potter, and Khnemu formed man upon his wheel. He created Thoth, the scribe, and Thoth opened the minds of men and taught them to read and write. All in all, nine gods were regarded as the highest, and the Sun was reverenced as the eye of the supreme god. In Heliopolis, the City of the Sun, the Creator of the Universe was known by the name of Tem.

Legend has it that the Sun-eye once ran away from her master into the Nubian Desert and there became a fearful lioness. Tem sent his scribe, wise Thoth, to persuade her to return. The lioness growled and bristled, but Thoth was not afraid, and finally succeeded in appealing to her better nature and making her realize the

62

Khnemu forming a man and his ka *on the potter's wheel*

essing of being the Sun-eye of Egypt. She went along with the
d's emissary, cooled her senseless anger in the cataract of the
le, and when she passed through various cities, assumed the
rm of a beautiful goddess, under which form she was thenceforth
orshipped. The Sun-eye became a wild beast a second time when
en rebelled against Tem, the Creator. This time the god him-
lf sent out his eye as the lioness-goddess Sekhet, in order to pun-
h unruly man. Sekhet killed thousands and drank their blood.
em, taking pity on humanity, called Sekhet back. But her fierce
stincts had been awakened and on the following day she wanted
wipe out the remainder of the human race. Therefore Tem had
ven thousand jugs of beer brewed, and mixed red paint into the
ink. Next morning, when Sekhet wanted to continue her murder-
us career, she found a knee-high lake of red beer before her.
hinking it human blood, she drank it until she became too drunk

to seek her prey. Thus the race of men was saved by the very go
against whom they had rebelled.

In the beginning, it is said, the earth was void, covered by water
just as the Egyptians found it year after year during the summer
time. The waters receded and a first mound began to rise up, the
glorious hill of the Earliest Days. In the mud of this hill sat eigh
spirits guarding an egg which lay on top of the hill. It broke oper
and a golden falcon emerged and winged its way into the heavens
From the Isle of the Flaming Dawn the winged sun arose—an
darkness no longer ruled the earth.

Of all the tales of the gods, the one that meant the most to th
ancient Egyptians was the story of Osiris, who was killed by hi
brother Set and who rose again to a new life. Geb, god of the earth
and Nut, goddess of the heavens, had two sons, Osiris and Set, an
two daughters, Isis and Nephthys. Isis and Osiris became one cou
ple and Nephthys and Set another. Set received the desert and th
sky above it for his portion, Osiris the Nile and the fruit-bearing
earth. Osiris became king over Egypt, and was so good a rule
that all loved him. But Set envied his brother and resolved to kil
him. He had a handsome box made, just large enough for Osi
ris, who was taller than all others. Then, when Osiris had invite
him to a banquet, he brought the chest with him, and a band c
conspirators as well. He promised the splendid chest to the on
whom it fitted exactly. When Osiris tried it, Set quickly closed th
lid, and the conspirators threw the chest into the Nile. Osiri
drowned, and was carried away by the current. His unhappy wif
Isis wandered over all the earth until at last she found the dea

Opposite: *The high priest Ptahhotep at the tabl*

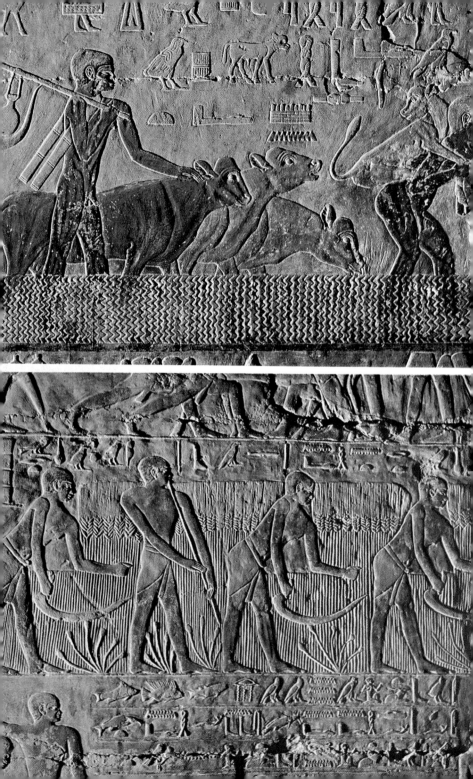

Anubis

Osiris. Then she broke out into lamentations: "Come to your house, you whose heart stands still. Gods and men turn their faces unto you. I call to you until my voice is heard unto Heaven!"

Then Anubis, the god who reigns on the threshold between the here and the hereafter, wrapped the body in mummy bands and buried it. But after Osiris' death Isis bore a son who was named Horus. When Set sought to kill the child of Osiris also, Isis hid him in the thickets of reeds in the delta. When Horus was grown, he met his father's murderer. They fought. Set fell, but Horus lost an eye. Thoth, the god of wisdom, placed this eye upon Osiris' heart, which was then given sight, and Osiris saw that another life existed. The resurrected Osiris became king in the land of the Western Ones, where men go after death. The living Horus, however, assumed the rulership of Egypt, and henceforth every Pharaoh was known as Living Horus as long as he wore the crown of the two lands. When he moved to the land of the Western Ones, he became Osiris.

Opposite: *Cattle led through water; tomb of Tiy in Saqqara* (above);
Reapers, flute players; tomb of Mereruka in Saqqara (below)

These various aspects of the Pharaoh are illustrated on an ancient palette, a stone tablet such as the Egyptians used for grinding face paint. Above, we see a falcon with an outstretched human hand. The emblem beneath represents his conquered enemies whom he holds in check. This is the Living Horus who reigns on earth and possesses mysterious powers. Another guise of the Living Horus is shown in the centre of the palette. Here he is represented as a man from whose belt hangs the tail of an animal. Primeval chieftains have also been represented in this way; the tail of the animal was a powerful magic, worn when ritual dances were performed before the paintings of animals in dark caves. By such ceremonies it was possible to win power over game animals.

Certainly the Pharaoh was represented with all kinds of super-

The Narmer palette, cosmetic palette of the First Dynasty

natural attributes. There are early pictures in which the Pharaoh's standards have hands that reach out for his enemies' hair. Or else the king is shown as a raging lion or a snorting bull. In the imagination of the people, the Pharaoh was a being as uncanny as the forces over which he was supposed to reign.

In fact, however, the Pharaoh had a perfectly rational function. His job was to harness the energies of his people and make out of the Egyptian swamp an orderly country of canals, fields, capital cities, and temples, with dwelling places for the present life and for eternity. The conditions under which the Egyptians lived were a challenge to human intelligence. The civilization of which the Pharaohs were the head developed amazing techniques for dealing with swampland, desert, and flood. In order to have water for their fields throughout the year, the Egyptians had to build dams, canals, and irrigation ditches. They observed the stars and learned to read in the heavens the time of the flood's beginning. They learned to survey the fields, for boundaries were wiped out by the river every year. They developed forms of writing and reckoning, and divided up their land into provinces: the Province of the Gazelle, the Province of the Hare, the Oldest Land, the Province of the Sycamores, and so on.

The two lands were thus divided up into forty-two provinces. Canal diggers, dike builders, astronomers, Great Seers—that is, priests—scribes, judges, teachers, architects, physicians, all stood in the employ of the Pharaoh. Every year the Pharaoh renewed the covenant he had made with the Nile. A scroll reminding the river of its duties was cast into the waters, together with sacrifices which were intended to put the Nile into a kindly mood.

The river also favoured the growth of trade. Ships were built and sailed down the Nile as far as the sea, and even across the sea to bring back lumber, gold, and precious stones. The Nile became the highway of Egypt. Compared to it, other roads were of such minor importance that for thousands of years it did not occur to the Egyptians to build wheeled wagons. They and their goods went about in boats; the dead were consigned to boats; in the Sun Boat the Pharaoh traversed the sky.

So strong was their sense of accomplishment that the Pharaoh's people felt themselves to be the greatest of all nations. The Egyptians looked down with contempt upon Nubians, Libyans, and Asiatics. They alone, they thought, deserved the name of men.

Old Kingdom ship for long voyages. In front of the cabin stands the ship's master, to whom the scribe is reporting

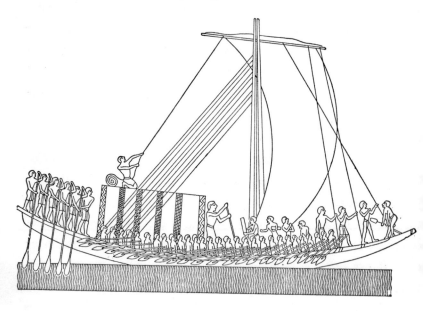

Their kings were sons of the Sun, in whose hand the ordering of the world had been placed.

Thoth, the god of wisdom, had taught the kings the art of calendar-making. The Egyptian year began with the day the Sothis, which we call Sirius, the Dog Star, appeared for the first time in the sky earlier than the sun. To the ancient Egyptians, this was a sign from heaven that the Nile would begin to rise. The Nile flood lasted for forty days; then the waters began to recede. On the twenty-sixth day in the fourth flood month, the king gave the command that Apis, the sacred bull, was to be driven around the White Walls of Memphis. This made the fields fertile and the sowing began. The people sang songs and wore strings of onions around their necks. Four months later the Pharaoh initiated the harvest by cutting the first swath of grain.

The Pharaoh was therefore in control of the basic rhythms of Egyptian agriculture. This was still another way in which he saw that the will of the gods was done on earth. As the guardian of righteousness, he had a special name—Maat. Other names for the Pharaoh were Living Falcon, Strong Bull, and Star in the Land of Light. Such was his eternal concern for his people that even after he had passed over into the Land of the Western Ones, he influenced the gods to look with favour upon the land of Egypt.

The Pharaoh was even supposed to know the sources of the Nile, and the secret of making it rise. It is said that Imhotep, the architect who built the first pyramid, revealed these secrets to the Pharaoh. Imhotep is also supposed to have added five additional days to the Egyptian year, bringing the number to 360 days—these days being the birthdays of the five children of Heaven and Earth: Set and Nephthys, Osiris and Isis, and Horus. Even after thousands of years his memory was still so much alive that the Greeks, when they came to Egypt, identified him with their god of medicine. He is the only man whose name was ever immortalized upon the stone statue of a Pharaoh.

Megdi studied the gleaming White Walls with which Imhotep had surrounded the world's first pyramid, as he and his father walked the last short distance across the desert.

"With Imhotep," Father was saying, "the age of the pyramid builders began. Unlike the ancient houses which were built from mud, the tombs and temples were constructed with more durable materials. Egypt was rich in variegated stone. At Tura a white limestone was quarried, at Aswân red and black granite, in Middle Egypt yellow-streaked alabaster; in Hammamat black and green basalt, porphyry, and cornelian, and in the Nubian Desert grey-green diorite. The Sinai Desert had depostis of turquoise much prized for jewellery. Statues large and small were fashioned out of stone—not only effigies of the Pharaoh and the nobles, but innumerable animal figures. The Egyptians seemed, at all phases of their history, to have a special love for animals and to celebrate them in their art.

"Even today we are stirred by the wonder of these pyramids which rimmed the desert. These great peaks, conceived by the awakening human spirit, rose up toward the sky to show the Sun where its sons on earth ruled. In building the pyramids the people elevated their Pharaoh, and in elevating the Pharaoh they uplifted themselves. They were enthusiastic and cheerful as they bent their backs to the tremendous labour needed to build these monuments."

Father pointed to the impressive gatehouse as he acknowledged the salute of the gaffer at the gate of Zoser's tomb. The stone was cut to imitate small clay bricks, and inside its walls the buttresses which formed indentations along both sides copied the shape of tremendous bundles of reeds. Father called Megdi's attention to the supports of the roof and the open doors: all were of durable stone.

They passed into the huge court and approached the six-step pyramid, the heart of the tremendous complex of buildings which covers an area of 900 by 1800 feet. The pyramid had been stripped of its gleaming limestone mantle, but had lost little of its size thereby. Father explained that its core was a mastaba similar to those which had been provided for the first Pharaohs: for King Serpent, King Scorpion, and King Fighting Falcon—Pharaohs of the first two dynasties who had performed the work of unifying the two lands.

"The actual tomb for Zoser was placed at a depth of one hundred feet," Father explained. "The architect Imhotep had it lined with Aswân granite and sealed with a block of granite weighing three and a half tons. Under the pyramid he created a labyrinth of corridors and rooms, an underground palace whose walls were panelled with green glazed tiles—copying the reed-mat work regularly used for covering mud brick walls—only this tiled reed would last to eternity. Stone vessels of exceptional beauty were placed in many of the chambers. Some vases must have been very costly, since it took an artist many weeks, or even many months, to hollow and grind them into shape."

Names of Upper Egyptian provinces in hieroglyphics: From left to right: Throne of Horus, Nubian Land, Jackal Province, Snake Province, Double Sceptre Province, Province of the Feminine Soul, Province of the Hare

Father showed Megdi that in addition to the granite tomb there was another grave to the south in which, apparently, the king's internal organs had been buried separately. Then he led the way to a massive stone structure, built somewhat like a blockhouse against the northern flank of the pyramid. Two round holes the same distance apart as human eyes had been made in the front wall. Peering through a window in the side wall, Megdi saw a head wearing a strange hood. The face was rather battered, lacking half its nose and eyes, yet it had a compelling dignity. It was a perfect replica of the statue of King Zoser, which was now housed in the Cairo museum. Here in the *serdab,* the sentry-box at the foot of the pyramid, the stone effigy of the king had stood sentinel for thousands of years, alert and ready to receive his *ka,* his spiritual essence, if it should desire to be a guest upon the earth for a while.

For to the mind of the ancient Egyptians, it was perfectly natural for the king to make a visit of inspection to his land, even after his death. The king still watched and worked over his people, though he was already in the Land of the Western Ones. Yet it was also of the greatest importance that the living ruler who sat upon the throne of the Pharaohs should have no weaknesses. After thirty years of reign every king was required to prove that he still had the

Names of Lower Egyptian provinces in hieroglyphics: From left to right: Busiris, Seventeenth Province, Second Province, The Inviolate Sceptre, Harpoon Province, Ibis Province, Point of the Fishes

strength to guide his people. This was done at the renewal festival, the *hebsed,* which had its roots in an age-old custom which has survived until the present in some African tribes: If a king loses his physical strength, he is killed and replaced by a new ruler, lest the entire people should become weak through their king.

The *hebsed* was evidently a development of this idea, the king being symbolically rejuvenated and reinvigorated. The ceremony took place before all the nobles of the kingdom, who represented the gods who waited upon the supreme god, Pharaoh. One of the nobles, acting the part of the god Thoth, presented the Pharaoh with an elixir of youth. Thereupon the king ran a race to prove his fitness to continue holding the reins of government.

The *hebsed* court lay between the north and the south palaces. The strange stone stumps in the great court had apparently served as pedestals for the thrones of Upper and Lower Egypt and had been the goals for the king's ritual race.

Then Father and Megdi entered the southern tomb where there were three paintings showing King Zoser running the *hebsed* race. "See, Megdi, how lightly the Pharaoh runs. He wears his crown and girdle and seems to dance under the Horus falcon which holds the key of life above his head. During his reign on earth Pharaoh was

73

'the Great God' who invited the other gods to visit him and conferred gifts upon them. He was the mightiest of all. Whenever Pharaoh appeared, he was preceded by the cry: Earth, beware your god comes!

"An incident which was related for thousands of years afterwards illustrates the unquestioning belief in Pharaoh's divine nature during the age of the pyramids. It seems that a high dignitary who walked close beside Pharaoh during a parade was accidentally touched by the king's staff. Everyone, including Pharaoh himself, expected the official to fall to the ground dead. To save the unfortunate man from such a fate, Pharaoh hastily pronounced a blessing which was miraculously efficacious, for the man did not fall dead after all.

"Such was the power of the kings for whom the pyramids were built as eternal residences."

Sign of Isis

Sign for ka

A VISIT TO NOBLE LORDS

"What about Pharaoh's officials?" Megdi wanted to know, as they passed through the high gate in the White Walls and out into the desert again. "Did they have fancy tombs, too?"

"The closer a man stood to the king," Father replied, "the greater the wealth that was lavished upon his tomb. All high officials were given eternal dwellings, and since the afterlife was to be longer than their life on earth, these tombs were far more splendid than the houses in which they spent their lifetimes. The wonderful thing about these graves is how they are filled with life. We have the expression: silent as the grave. But these graves of Egypt are far from silent. In fact, they tell us more of the life of ancient Egypt, in all its details, than you might believe possible. The walls of the tombs are covered with pictures in which the life of officials, artisans, shepherds, artists, and peasants, has been immortalized. The men who were buried in those tombs expected to go on living, and they took the world as they knew it down into their tombs with them.

"Let us pay a call on the tombs of Lords Ptahhotep, Mereruka, and Ti. These are the most informative of all that have been dug out of the sands of Saqqara."

It was only a few minutes' walk to the eternal home of Lord Ptahhotep. Down a few steps, through a door in the rock—and Megdi stood face to face with the highest-ranking pyramid priest of King Asosi's reign.

"That is Lord Ptahhotep," Father said, pointing to a seated figure that took up a large part of one wall. The way he sits on his lion-legged chair, the way he carries his head and holds his hands, indicates clearly enough that he is conscious of his dignity. In addition to the wide collar and knee-length apron, he wears a leopard skin, a special garment reserved for high priests. Lord Ptahhotep holds a long list of offices. And he also enjoys one of the largest shares in the many joys that Pharaoh brings to the land of the Nile, for scarcely anyone stands closer to Pharaoh than his highest priest.

"See how Ptahhotep is stretching out his right hand to the table in front of him. It is laden with delicacies; roast goose, fish cake, ham, and who knows what other dainties in those covered bowls. With his left hand he is raising to his nose an ointment vessel which is inscribed: 'Finest Festival Fragrance Oil.' Under the table more supplies stand in readiness, as well as fruits and flowers— blue water lilies and lotus blossoms. Under the chair crouches a figure which has been almost effaced. Evidently it represented someone who had lost Lord Ptahhotep's favour forever. 'I no longer want to see this person!' he said one day, and so the person became only a shadow."

Father took Megdi into another tomb. "This belongs to a grand vizier," he said. He was the Pharaoh's chief administrator. Obviusly he is getting ready for the day ahead of him. Servants hasten to dress him. One carefully places a wig on his head, so that his face will have a dignified frame. Another tends to his feet, another to his clothes. Four dwarfs are busy arranging his collar, which is an important sign of his rank. The foreman of the menagerie stands behind his master holding his favourite monkeys and three dogs on leashes. Two officials stand near, looking very conscientious and busy as they await their master's instructions. The one who has succeeded in taking a position in front hands over a papyrus scroll. In the background harp and flute players make music, and the chief scenter tests the fragrance of the fruit which is to be served at the breakfast table, to determine whether it is choice enough for the great lord. Everything is arranged to put the vizier in a good mood. He is addressed by the long litany of his titles, presented with lists containing staggering accounts of his possessions: tens of thousands of oxen, gazelles, poultry, jugs of beer, breads. Servants carry in bales of linen, bundles of sandals, boxes of utensils, cosmetics, incense—the ancient Egyptians believed that clouds of incense would form a bridge to heaven. But blessedness is conceived in terms of earthly things. Tenderly, a little girl holds up flowers. But the master's eye prefers to rest upon his son, still a child, who has two reed pens tucked behind his ear, one for red and one for black ink, and carries a roll of papyrus in his hand—his father's pride and joy, a little scribe who already has some knowledge of the high art of hieroglyphics.

"After the day's work has been assigned, the vizier makes an inspection of his estates, accompanied by his wife and daughters. A small boy runs alongside, a bird in his hand—it is the kind called a hoopoe. Baboons are also taken along, and one of the sly rascals unexpectedly bites his keeper in the leg, much to the amusement of the others. With satisfaction the landowner observes how industriously his men are working, keeping wells and canals in order, cutting the tall barley, and tending the livestock. Geese and cranes are being fattened; they twist their necks and try to resist the noodles being crammed into their open beaks.

"Two field workers are caught in a pasture secretly milking a cow. 'Hurry, the herdsman is coming!' one urges the other. But it is already too late. Punishment follows quickly, a regular rain of blows.

"Down by the canal fists are flying too, but not on orders from above. Some sailors have become involved in a brawl. They flail away, and one of them shouts: 'Break his head open—there's not much in it anyhow.'

"Evidently the life of herdsmen and sailors, artisans and farmers, is not a smooth one, but still they season it with grim humour. The litter-bearers who carry their master—for a man of his dignity only rarely allows his artfully embroidered sandals to touch the naked earth—sing as they toil: 'We would rather have the litter full than empty.' And with a glance at the stick their overseer carries, the litter-bearers remark: 'That is the club with which my back is anointed.'

"Shepherds who have the task of driving their herds from one pasture to another through flood waters test the slippery ground with their crooks, and one murmurs: 'How fitting for herdsmen to visit the fish and ask after their health.'

"The farmers in the Nile marshes are rough-looking fellows who not seem to be too badly off. They carry many a goose inside their own stomachs instead of to the market. Their youngsters behave like young ruffians. Rough-and-tumble games and tussles are common; you can see one boy being tossed right over another's head. But when they are called to work they pretend to have no idea what it is all about. 'Sebkai, bring the cord,' a farmer calls to his son; he wants to tie up a boatload of bundled reeds. The heavy rope is still in his hut. But what does the boy bring? A thread that his mother might use for sewing! 'This is what you wanted, isn't it?' he asks with the most innocent expression, and the father drives the little prankster away.

"Here's another amusing riverside spectacle. Cowherds are trying to drive their cattle across the water. But the cows evidently do not think much of the magic spells one of the herdsmen has pronounced to frighten away the lurking crocodiles. Then one man takes a calf on his back and courageously carries it into deeper water, whereupon the cow splashes after her baby, and the other cows follow her."

"There are so many things going on that I can't keep up with them!" Megdi exclaimed.

"Yes, wherever we look we see a variegated, bustling life. Here fish are being dried, there grapes harvested, and here the vintners are treading the grapes with bare feet. Here barley or wheat is cut and threshed by the hoofs of donkeys. Rams are being driven over fields planted with the second sowing of the year; the sharp hoofs of the animals will drive the grain into the soft earth.

"Carpenters saw logs to make boards for furniture, stonemasons hew blocks, potters shape jugs on their wheels. Serving maids work

79

the hand mills to grind grain, calling out to one another: 'A litt
faster, if you can!' To which the reply comes: 'I am working
fast as I can.'

"You can almost hear the noise and tumult in the market plac
Cakes are being vended: 'Fine cakes, still hot!' 'Linen, sandal
first-class goods!' 'How much is a jug of oil?' A hundred shouts an
cries ring out at once.

"The vizier sees all this and is content. He rejoices in the rollicl
ing life of his country; he loves this din, which is the echo of h
good government. Sometimes he enters a boat and is rowed to th
papyrus thickets where the hippos bask in the mud. The hipp
bulls are hunted with harpoons and ropes. The vizier's wife
in the boat with the party. Anxiously, she holds her husband firml
by one leg when he hurls the harpoon. It is a dangerous sport, fc
the wounded animals rage and turn upon everything within sigh
An aroused hippopotamus will bite a crocodile in two, his teet
cutting right through the armour at first bite."

"Is all this activity on the margins a part of the hippo hunt?
Megdi asked, peering closely at the figures depicted there.

"Yes, they show what is happening in the area at the same time
For example: ichneumon and wildcat plundering birds' nests, an
a kingfisher swooping down upon its victim. Frightened by th
shouts and bellowing, a baby hippopotamus attempts to clim
upon its mother's back. The reeds and caves along the shore an
also a paradise for bird hunters. Crooked throwing-sticks muc
like Australian boomerangs whirr into the frightened flocks, th
sharp edges breaking the birds' wings or necks. On land, nets an

Opposite: *Sarcophagus chamber in the Unas pyrami*

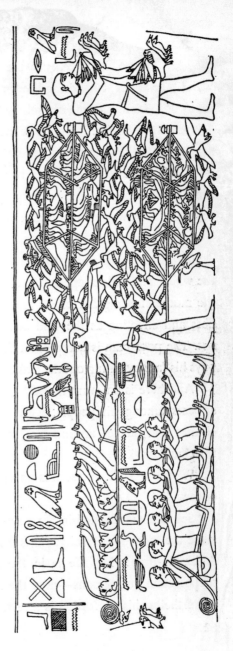

Catching birds with drawnets (from the tomb of Ptahhotep)

Opposite: *Amenemhet III (Twelfth Dynasty), represented as a maned sphinx*

decoys are set up. Once the flock has fallen into the nets, the bird catchers, at a prearranged signal, pull so violently at the strings that they fall flat on their backs in the grass. The nets clap shut. The vizier takes delight in seeing the thrashing birds and estimates how many of these toothsome morsels he has captured.

"When he returns home he is met by his hunters, whom he has sent out into the desert. They are bringing their prey home in cages —jackals and hyenas, and even two lions. The greyhound and leopards which have done the major part of the hunting for the men are scored with claw marks. Gazelles and ibexes are part of the hunters' bag. Small sidelights, too, are recorded on the walls of the tombs. A hedgehog is just about to catch a locust. Swallows circle about the walls. The little shepherd carrying a lamb across the canal, and the mother feeding her child, are observed with the same carefulness and affection as the wild duck that draws its foot out of the net. The poor man is taken upon the ferry that crosses the Nile; he pays his fare by baling out the leaky boat.

"And here is an event that does not happen every day: Pharaoh appears among his people. Everyone throws off his sandals and clothes and dances around him, sending up shrill cries of joy to the cloudless sky.

"Wherever we look there is an outpouring of life like the waters of the Nile!

"See that man seated in the corner? He is the one who will preserve the scene for eternity. He is the chief sculptor, whose name is Ankh-ma-Ptah: 'My life is in the hand of Ptah.' Not the most prepossessing of persons—note the shining bald spot on his head. Nevertheless his profession is a rewarding one: he enjoys the good

The chief sculptor (from the tomb of Ptahhotep)

things of life. He dines as he cruises down the river in a pleasure barge. Roast fowl is served to him, and figs and cakes. The covered bowls no doubt contain all sorts of hot delicacies, the full pitchers choice beverages.

"The vizier, whose imperishable house the sculptor has filled with life, has treated him well. The craftsmen who worked under Ankh-ma-Ptah may be paid in bread and beer, linen and ointments, barley and wheat; but something more than crumbs from the table of his master falls to the lot of the chief sculptor.

"Here is a solemn scene. The members of the king's council are being led before the Pharaoh. First comes the man chosen for the highest office. The Pharaoh speaks: 'Behold, your office is not sweet but bitter. The vizier is the copper wall that surrounds the king's golden house. To all who stand high, princes and dignitaries, your ear shall be the same and your eye the same as to those whose tables are empty and who own only one apron. And when a man with debts appears before you, tear up half of the note the debtor has given, and cast it away. For you stand in a public place; wind and water speak of you. What you do cannot remain hidden. Remember that a man lives on after his death. His deeds will be heaped up like mountains beside him!'

"Summarizing his brilliant career, the noble owner of the tomb affirms: 'Everyone who worked for me was content. I gave bread to the hungry, filled the shores with cattle; I gave even to the wolves of the mountain and the birds of the sky.' "

"That would be quite a record," Megdi commented. "If it were true."

Father, who had been leading him from picture to picture, was of the same opinion. "If we were to take all these inscriptions at their word," he said, "ancient Egypt must have been a paradise on earth. That it was not. But such statements do make it plain that the Egyptians of the Old Kingdom had consciences. They were people who thought about their social responsibilities. As long ago as that, people had realized that man has a higher goal than just maintaining himself in an inhospitable world. Not that they hadn't mastered that part of it. They paid their debt to the soil that the Nile gave them year after year. Working together as one great family, they transformed the valley of the Nile into a garden. But they did even more than this: they made the attempt to overcome perishability and fear of death. Instead of speaking of dying, the Egyptians used such words as: go across, anchor, land, rise again, cross the Lake of the Lotus, enter the land in which nothing is mute. In a barge steered by the ferryman named 'Backward looking' the departed soul crossed the eternal Nile.

"The ancients thought of the human soul as having wings like a bird. Hence, it was customary for people to plant trees in whose branches, they imagined, their soul-bird, the *ba,* could perch. The *ka,* which held the essence of the person, was freed at death of the fetters which bound it to the body, but it might choose at any time to come back to the body to seek refuge. Therefore the body must be protected from decay. They were masters of the art of embalming. In fact, we cannot think of Egypt without thinking of mummies. So much was mummification central to the civilization of Egypt that the ancient Egyptians traced it back to their beloved Osiris, 'the first of the Western Ones,' who was made into a mummy by Anubis. The art was taken over by the Egyptians themselves, who certainly brought it to high perfection. So much so that innumerable mummies have come through the centuries so well preserved that their features and even their facial expressions can be seen clearly.

"In order to be on the safe side, the more privileged of the Egyptians also had a stone body, a statue, made for their tombs. This statue was installed in the *serdab,* that little sentry-box like the one you saw attached to King Zoser's pyramid. Through the spy holes the deceased watched the gifts that were brought to him: food and drink, clothing, anointing oil, furniture, hunting gear, and weapons. Through the spy holes he could take in music, fresh air, and light. He was separated from those he had left behind only by an illusory door. They were required to continue taking care of him. In many a man's will, the produce of whole villages was

85

set aside for his provisioning after death. But for insurance against human carelessness, the prudent man would order sculptors and painters to wield their spells so that everything he would need in the afterlife would appear on the walls of his tomb. In this way the master of the grave was supplied for ever, and was independent of the outside world. He had a band of servants with him, who would attend to every necessity. He had his kinfolk with whom he could continue to lead a happy family life. By this artistic device he forestalled the forgetfulness of those who would come after. Even if the visits and the offerings ceased, he was provided against loneliness and want. Even if the desert sands were to block the entrance to his house, they could not smother the life that lined the walls of those deeply hidden chambers. Thousands of years later archaeologists brought that life back into the light of day again."

Father and Megdi went up a few steps of the short stairway leading from the tomb, and the lingering image of the wall paintings was blotted out by the glare of the noonday sun upon the desert. Megdi blinked into that overwhelming brightness. He started. About twenty yards away, he saw an old man in a blue *galabia* coming toward them. Could it be—was it really—Gurgar?

"Did you tell him to meet us here?" Megdi asked.

"He would have known we were here even if I hadn't said a word," Father whispered back. "He has his way of knowing what I'm about. Besides, he's made up his mind to enlist you, and that is all there is to it."

Father greeted Gurgar as though he had been expecting him. "High time you got here. Half an hour later and you would have found us well-nigh starved to death." And at these words Megdi suddenly remembered that it had been a long time since breakfast.

"Suppose we go to Mariette's house," his father went on, laughing. "All those wonderful pictures of foodstuffs—even after all these centuries, they make my mouth water."

IN MARIETTE'S HOUSE

As was usual at noon, tourists from every part of the globe were converging from the various points of interest toward the spreading house whose terrace afforded a view over the tombs of Saqqara as far as the pyramid of Zoser. Besides the tourists were the usual swarm of dragomans, camel drivers, and muleteers, with their animals. It turned out that Megdi's father had already reserved a table for them in the restaurant. It was pleasantly cool in the big room. Dark-faced Nubians in white *galabias* waited on the guests. During their lunch Megdi noticed that Gurgar listened with the closest attention to every word that Father said. Finally the conversation came around to Mariette. Father expressed his great admiration for the man. Gurgar, to Megdi's surprise, took issue with this.

"Who else has found what he has?" Father countered. "No, he was phenomenal. Wherever he started to dig—at Giza and Saqqara, Abydos and Idfu, Karnak, Dai al-Bahri and Biban el Muluk—he uncovered treasures. We are still working over his sites."

"Oh yes, he had a lucky touch," Gurgar admitted grudgingly. "I know all about that. My uncle helped him when he was at the peak of his career, and I have heard a good many stories about Mariette from Uncle."

"Could I hear one?" Megdi asked impulsively. His curiosity had been aroused by this controversy between Father and Gurgar.

Gurgar was not at all reluctant. "Ah, Mariette, Mariette," he began. Whatever grudge Gurgar might have against the long-dead archaeologist did not spoil his zest in telling a story about him. "He was a clever one. Boat after boat went down the Nile to Alexandria, loaded with boxes of precious things he had found. Everything was going to France. Naturally. In those days we had no laws to keep foreigners from taking away our treasures.

"In those days Egypt was ruled over by a khedive. By and by the khedive heard what the Frenchman was doing. He sent a major to Saqqara, where Mariette was digging. Piles of boxes stood ready for shipment. The major tapped them suspiciously. Mariette remained as cool as you please. He welcomed the major and informed him that he had come on a fortunate day. 'Yesterday,' Mariette told him, 'we were working in a shaft grave and ran into a treasure-trove of gold that surpasses anything we have found yet.'

"The major's eyes sparkled. 'Where is the gold?' he demanded. 'I want to see that place at once.' Mariette readily led him to the shaft grave. The major descended a rope ladder to the bottom of the shaft, some hundred feet below the ground. He was no sooner at the bottom than Mariette pulled up the rope ladder. 'What is the meaning of this?' the major stormed. 'Where is the gold?'

" 'Up here and packed away,' Mariette replied. He let down a

89

basket with enough food and water to last the poor major fo twenty-four hours. He himself went back to his work, preparing th boxes for shipment down the Nile. By the following day the kh dive's envoy had stopped ranting and raging, and was willing t negotiate. What else could he do? Could he go back to the khediv and confess that he, a son of the Nile, had been tricked by a fo eigner?

"Mariette made an offer: 'Half of everything that is excavate in the future will be for the excavators, that is, for the museum i Paris; and half for the khedive, that is, for the museum in Cairo.'

" 'But there is no museum in Cairo,' the major objected.

" 'Then the khedive ought to build one,' Mariette said.

"The major seemed not entirely content. Mariette—oh but h was a shrewd one—knew what was needed. 'And a little from eac half,' he expanded his offer, 'for the khedive's excellent major That was how he did things, your Mariette."

Megdi and his father laughed. "He was a realist," Father saic "He worked within the framework of the time and place."

But Gurgar still shook his head. "He was a fox," he said, "t carry away all the treasures that belong to us."

"But for him you would not have the Cairo museum," Megdi father reminded Gurgar.

"He was full of tricks," Gurgar continued to grumble.

"He had to be, to accomplish his purposes."

"A perfidious Frenchman," Gurgar persisted.

"He loved Egypt," Father countered, "as few men have eve done. Don't forget. It was a hundred years ago, and not man foreigners came to Egypt then. Mariette was sent by the museum

Paris to buy papyrus rolls for their collection. Once he had set ot in this land, he was caught and held by its spell. He stayed on nd became as much a native as the Stone Age hunters from the ahara, the immigrants from Nubia and the Near East, or the con-uerors from Libya, Persia, Macedonia, Rome, and Arabia. Vhatever they were, wherever they came from—as soon as they ad stayed here a little while, they became Egyptians. The same ing happened to Mariette. Of course he sent much of what he und back to France. Only in France, in those days, were there e learned men who could make sense of what had been dug out f the sands. And what a brilliant instinct he had. Almost all the tes in Egypt where archaeologists are toiling today are places Iariette first opened up. And that one hundred years ago! He was ne of the truly great figures of the pioneer days of archaeology, a an who went to work with virtually nothing but his bare hands, ke Denon or Belzoni."

These names only made Gurgar frown the blacker, Megdi oticed. "Denon!" the old man said scornfully. "Belzoni!"

"I know what you mean," Megdi's father retorted. "You are inking of the mounds of shards that still remind us of Belzoni's urried work, of the royal tombs that he broke open with battering ams. Of course. All those pioneers in archaeology were destructive. grant that. It was only natural; they were beginners. And that is eir greatness: that they did make a beginning. Think of all they ad to put up with: hunger and thirst, filth and sickness, open nd hidden threats. From whom? From Egyptians who had only ne end in view, and that was to keep the treasures for themselves nd convert them into cash. It happened more than once that the

91

first diggers were actually attacked by marauding bands. The braved gunfire. They overcame staggering difficulties. For the knew that what they were doing was important. They were di covering things that had been neglected and forgotten in the so of Egypt for three or four or five thousand years. No short-sighte native of that day and age—who wanted to peddle an antique two—would have known how to proceed. Those were inspire men, Gurgar. They risked their lives for their task."

"Did they really?" Megdi asked, more than a little thrilled.

"Take a man like Giovanni Battista Belzoni, for example," F ther continued. "In March, 1818, he broke into the pyramid Chephren. His helpers were afraid to follow him down the narro shafts, but Belzoni kept on, crawling through passages where th air was almost unbreathable and the roof threatened to fall i When his path was blocked by rubble, he scooped it away with h bare hands, until at last he reached the burial vault itself and stoo before the sarcophagus of Chephren. Belzoni was utterly fearles You might call him a great adventurer, except that he had a genu ine passion for ancient Egypt.

"Was he French, too?" Megdi asked.

"No, Italian," Father replied. "He came from a good family Rome and was supposed to become a monk. But the quiet lif of a monastery was not for a young man of his powerful buil and active temperament. He became involved in political conspira cies and had to flee to England in order to escape imprisonmen There he earned his living for a time as a side-show 'giant,' liftin and tossing iron weights about as if they were footballs. But Belzon had a good mind as well as a strong body. He spent his nights study

g engineering and, incidentally, reading everything he could find
out the Land of the Pharaohs. His engineering studies quickly
ok a practical turn, and he invented a mechanical water wheel
hich would deliver four times as much water as the device then
. use in Egypt. Belzoni saved his side-show earnings and as soon
; he could finance the trip, he set off for Egypt. He wanted to
monstrate his new water wheel to the pasha."

"Tell the boy about the pasha," Gurgar suggested. These were
was evident, old stories to him, but he listened to them with rel-
h.

Father hesitated a moment. Then he said: "Very well. The pa-
a's name was Mohammed Ali, and he was not exactly the nicest
f men. He had been in the midst of a struggle for power with a
roup of Mameluke beys. Finally a compromise was agreed on,
nd Mohammed Ali invited 480 of his enemies to a great reconcil-
tion feast. As soon as they were all together, Ali's soldiers fell
pon them and slaughtered them to the last man."

"Oh!" Megdi gasped. "And this was the pasha Belzoni went to
sit?"

"As you might expect, our friend Belzoni did not receive a very
arm welcome. The pasha was thoroughly indifferent to the pos-
bility of improving the lot of his subjects with Belzoni's water
heel. But Belzoni was not the man to brood long over a disap-
ointment. Instead, he took a job with the British Consul-General
Cairo, a man named Salt who happened to be a great collector of
ntiques. It seems that there was a colossal statue of Ramses the
econd which Salt wanted transported from Luxor to Alexandria.
elzoni volunteered to do it. He was given the assignment, and

93

in spite of enormous difficulties, carried it out. Belzoni's succe[ss]
spurred him on to begin collecting for himself.

"For five years he snatched up everything that seemed to him [of]
any value, no matter how small or large. Scarabs, sarcopha[gi,]
statues, jewellery, even obelisks—he took everything."

Megdi's eyes widened. "What would he do with an obelisk?" [he]
wondered.

Father smiled. "He took it to England with him. He reasone[d]
that if the monument had been brought to its site, it could be take[n]
away again. Belzoni not only moved one of those colossal grani[te]
needles; he dropped it into the Nile by accident and managed [to]
fish it out again when everyone had given it up for lost. No tas[k]
seemed too formidable for him. He infected everyone under hi[m]
with his own courage and good humour. Perhaps that is how h[e]
managed to accomplish so much."

"Actually, what did he accomplish?" Megdi wanted to know.

"Well, for example, he discovered a whole series of tombs i[n]
the Valley of the Kings, including the tomb of Seti I, which la[y]
hidden deep inside the rocky cliff. In 1820 he put on an Egyptia[n]
exhibit in London. He showed a model of this tomb, with its won[-]
derful painted walls. Added to this was the Pharaoh's actual sarcoph[-]
agus, and any number of precious articles. The exhibit was a grea[t]
success. Belzoni felt that he had discovered all the secrets of th[e]
Valley of the Kings."

"He congratulated himself too early," Gurgar said drily. "We ar[e]
still making important finds there."

"So we are," Father said. "The Valley of the Kings seems in[-]
exhaustible. Only twenty-five years after Belzoni, a scholar fro[m]
94

ermany named Karl Richard Lepsius and his staff of scientists
nducted a three-year expedition that carried them all the way to
hiopia. It was a journey packed with excitement. They had ex-
cted to encounter hostility from some of the remote tribesmen,
t they were scarcely prepared for an onslaught of the elements.
ley were treated to the experience of a cloudburst on the Nile—
e sort of thing that happens once in decades. Floods carried away
eir tents and all their equipment. Nevertheless they stuck it out,
ent on with their work, and for the first time in archaeological his-
ry made a systematic coverage of the area they had chosen to
udy. They found the remains of thirty hitherto unknown pyramids,
d some 130 mastabas of the early dynasties.

"Unlike Belzoni, Lepsius was not self-taught; he was a trained
ientist, and he had the assistance of a team of experts. He went
out his work with considerable care, uncovering the ruins, ex-
mining them with skill and knowledge, and preserving a good
cord of what he came upon, both by written descriptions and ac-
urate sketches. One of the special accomplishments of this expedi-
on was the careful measurement of Biban el Muluk—or as the
nglish call it, the Valley of the Kings.

"When Lepsius returned to Europe, he had not only tangible
easures to take with him, but a wealth of knowledge and ideas.
that we can consider him one of the founders of Egyptology,
long with Champollion and Brugsch.

"But Mariette, too, was more than a lucky finder. He was a true
iscoverer, and a scholar of remarkable insight. Thousands of peo-
le before him had seen the sphinxes; thousands had passed by
le head of the Great Sphinx that rose from the desert sands at Saq-

qara. But Mariette was the first to see that all the scattered sphinxes were of the same type. He dug out one sphinx and went on digging until he had uncovered 141 sphinxes, and the bases of many more —revealing a great avenue of sphinxes. On November 12, 1851 Mariette found the entrance to the underground complex of which the sphinxes were only the markers. By the glow of torches a room passage was revealed, sealed by an enormous granite block. When this was pierced, the searchers found themselves in a series of chambers. In each chamber stood an immense sarcophagus (more than ten feet high, six feet wide and twelve feet long) with sides of polished black or red basalt. But every sarcophagus was empty. At last Mariette came upon a walled-up chamber. In it was one unrifled sarcophagus which contained the lavishly ornamented mummy of a bull! This was the cemetery for the holy Apis bulls which were led by the Pharaoh around the White Walls of Memphis each year to fertilize the soil before the sowing. In those tremendous tunnels there was room enough for eternal temples to whole dynasties of the huge beasts."

"Temples for bulls?" Megdi asked, somewhat shocked.

"Not only for bulls," Father said. "The ancient Egyptians revered the lion, the falcon, the ibis, the cat, the snake, the crocodile, the hippopotamus, the ichneumon, and the scarab. A man who killed a sacred animal incurred the death penalty. Such sinful killing, it was felt, mocked the god whose spirit lived in the animal. The bull was worshipped for its power to create new life; the lion and the snake were regarded as embodiments of divine wrath which is more terrible than the wind of the desert; the baboon was

Opposite: *Three musicians; tomb of Nak*

96

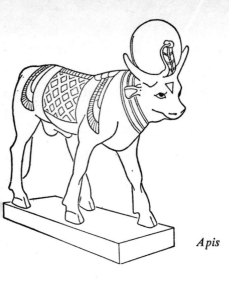

Apis

considered to be a vessel of divine wisdom. In temple writings we read 'the eye of the baboon traverses the Land of the Nile through all its breadth, and when it discovers that any man uses the writing of his fingers to cheat, it takes all nourishment from him.'

"In recent years investigators have found more than four million jars containing embalmed ibises, as well as countless cat mummies, some of them gilded. As for the beetles called scarabs, they were a special favourite of the Egyptians and served as good-luck pieces. Millions upon millions of scarab amulets were made, either from clay or precious stone, and worn around the neck or set into a ring. The scarab, which rolls a tiny ball of manure, then lays its egg in the ball, dies, and reappears again from the ball, was called by the ancients: 'He who rises out of himself.' They took scarab charms with them to the grave as a pledge of their own resurrection.

Opposite: *Young pilot; tomb of Menna in Qurna*

"The scarab, the phoenix, and the heavenly falcon were, to the Pharaoh's people, three different signs for the one Being who existed beyond the Sun and worked through it. When the Egyptian had moved into his eternal home, it did not matter whether the bread he ate took the form of actual baked bread, or bread carved out of stone, or bread in the form of written words. All these were guises for the fundamental bread. In the same way, birds and animals as they lived upon earth were regarded as images and transformations the gods had made of themselves.

"This is one of the basic mysteries of Egypt, and one which we moderns find hard to understand. For Mariette, the concept became clear when he found the tombs of the Apis bulls. It was all suddenly illuminated for him. Those early investigators had a clearer grasp of the ideas underlying the finds than was had by many who came after them. Perhaps it was because they had the benefit of fresh, uncluttered vision. Those that came after knew more, it is true, but their knowledge was a matter of detail.

"But to come back to Mariette: in the last months of his life he made one of his most important discoveries. He found pyramids with inscriptions, pyramids that could tell their own story."

"It was not Mariette who found them!" Gurgar protested with strong emotion. "It was two of his Egyptian workmen who first entered a pyramid in which the outer chambers had inscriptions on the walls."

"And were they able to read the hieroglyphics?"

"I helped them," Gurgar said with impassive face.

"Then you are the very person to show Megdi these pyramids," Megdi's father said. He glanced at his watch. "I have some matters to attend to in the neighbourhood. You and Megdi will have a nice time by yourselves, won't you? And we can meet again at five o'clock right here in the courtyard of the restaurant."

Father drove off in the car, and Gurgar and Megdi headed for a group of shapeless mounds which rose above the desert like rubbish heaps.

"Are those pyramids?" Megdi asked, a bit distrustfully.

"Those were pyramids, too," Gurgar replied. "And meant to be as proud as any pyramid constructed. But clouds were gathering over the realm of the Pharaohs when they were being built."

THE GREAT UPHEAVAL

They went first to the Unas pyramid. Gurgar and Megdi mounted the ramp up which the dead Pharaoh had been borne from the temple in the valley to his eternal home.

"Why is it called the Unas pyramid?" Megdi asked. "Was that the name of the king?"

"Unas," Gurgar told him, "was the last king of the Fifth Dynasty. Previously, the state had been like a firmly built human pyramid, with Pharaoh the golden apex, the pivot between heaven and earth. The rise and fall of the Nile, the prosperity of fields and all growing things, the orbits of the stars, had all been subject to the king's power. Pharaoh had been regarded as the Great House who sheltered Egypt. The Great Pyramid of Giza was the summation of that period and that point of view. Now, many changes took place in Egypt between the Fourth and Fifth Dynasty. But in the Fifth Dynasty a Pharaoh came along with new doctrines and a new religious emphasis. He did not lay stress on his own omnipotence, but on the fact that he and all his people were sons of the Sun God. He wanted to create sanctuaries to that great 'Father.' The size of the pyramids diminished, for the Pharaoh no longer asserted his unique supremacy. Instead, vast temples to the sun were built, whose characteristic motif was the obelisk.

"With the Pharaoh no longer so strong, powerful figures moved into the foreground: nobles, district commanders, viziers, and high priests. Bit by bit they seized control of the land, which had belonged to the king alone. After all, there were many such nobles, who were able to turn things to their own advantage: the 'guardians of the Diadem,' who exercised rule as Pharaoh's deputies; the 'guides of the palace,' through whose hands the government decrees passed; the 'privy councillors of the House of Morning,' who came to dress the Pharaoh every morning and give him their advice while doing so. These people were the 'eyes and ears of the king.' They had an army of lesser officials under them, and could control the operation of the government. As time went on, their number swelled. It became harder and harder for the common people of the realm to support this horde of parasitic officials. Nevertheless, they continued to grow in wealth and power, so much so that the Pharaohs elevated the officials' daughters to the status of royal consorts. Counts and viziers now had their sarcophagi made in the shape of palaces. The tombs of priests and other dignitaries became more costly and elaborate. All this display had to be bought by human labour. The people who had looked up to Pharaoh as to a father, whose welfare he was supposed to protect and advance, paid the price for this glory. Under Unas their condition became still more wretched. We find mention for the first time of 'millions'—equivalent to what we nowadays would call 'the masses.' "

Gurgar pointed out a block relief along the ramp. It showed a group of figures of unmistakable gauntness, people reduced to skin and bone. "As you see, there were famines. Here is the clearest evidence of the misery of the common people. The ancient sculptors were good and honest reporters. But let us now take a closer look at the pyramid."

From the outside the pyramid seemed scarcely worth bothering about. It was nothing but a shapeless mound of weather-beaten limestone, and Megdi said so.

"You are right," Gurgar said. "So little did it seem worth bothering about that it was not until 1881 that anyone found the entrance to the inner chambers. That was done by Sir Gaston Maspero, successor of Mariette. However, you will be surprised by what you see inside."

Gurgar was right, for Megdi was struck dumb with amazement. Gurgar had borrowed a flashlight from the gaffer at the entrance, and its beam revealed light-coloured walls surrounding a tremendous sarcophagus. Endless rows of hieroglyphics, chiselled into polished limestone blocks, were painted a blue that imitated the skies of Egypt.

It was very quiet in the chamber. Megdi looked at the clearly chiselled hieroglyphics. Here were messages that could not fade or be rubbed away. And suddenly a voice filled the room: "Rise up, King Unas. Take your head, assemble your limbs, shake the sand from your flesh! Bread that cannot mould has been served for you, beer that will never sour. A ramp of light has been laid under your feet. Mount upon it to the horizon. King Unas conquers the heavens and splits their gate of copper. He feeds upon spirits; it is King

102

Unas who eats their magic powers and takes their souls into himself. Unas is Osiris in the whirlwind. Unas marches in; he takes upon himself the power to decide and passes judgement over those who live in the Land of the Sun. The gods, wrapped in their garments, white sandals upon their feet, throw off clothes and sandals when you appear before them, and speak: 'Our hearts would not rejoice until you came. Behold, the god of all, whose eye is Sun and Moon, comes to receive you. You will spend the night in his arms like the infant calf in the arms of his herdsman!' "

The loud and solemn voice echoed and died away. Gurgar certainly knew how to read hieroglyphics, Megdi thought. He read them as well as Megdi could read his schoolbooks. It was all a little uncanny, and Megdi was rather glad when Gurgar led the way out into the light of day again.

Solar temple of King Niussere

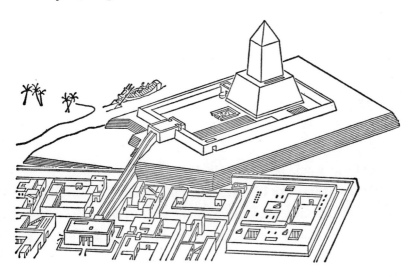

Now they climbed to the top of the pyramid, from which they had a good view of their surroundings. Gurgar pointed to another of the mounds of rubble. "That one is the pyramid of Pepi II," he told Megdi, "the king whose reign marked the end of the Old Kingdom. You will find texts and magic spells inside that pyramid also, much like those we saw in the pyramid of Unas. The texts aver that the king is stronger than death, mightier than all the gods, more powerful than heaven and earth. In the mortuary temple the Pharaoh is represented as conqueror of the hippopotamus, and in the passage to the inner sanctum of the temple he is shown as victor over his enemies. He has forced a prince of Libya to his knees, holds him by the hair, and is about to smash his head with a club. The prisoner's wife and two sons are pleading for mercy."

"He must have been a very strong Pharaoh," said Megdi, much impressed.

Gurgar laughed a wicked little laugh. "Jecquier, the archaeologist who spent ten years excavating this pyramid, made an interesting discovery: a picture just like this one may be found in the mortuary temple of Sahure, a king who reigned more than one hundred years before Pepi. Every single feature had been taken over, including the names of the Libyan prince, the wife and the sons. Pepi was taking credit for a victory which a former Pharaoh had won for Egypt."

"But why would he want to do that?" Megdi wondered.

"That was just like Pepi II," Gurgar replied. A strange look had come over his face. He looked absent and yet somehow more preoccupied. It almost seemed as though he were mulling over some ancient grudge.

104

"What do you mean?" Megdi pressed. "What do you mean, it was just like Pepi II?"

"Such a childlike trick," Gurgar explained. "He was six years old when he was raised to the throne, and he remained king until he passed into his second childhood. Ninety-four years he reigned, and in his whole reign nothing delighted him more than a certain dwarf. For the sake of this dwarf he had a long letter written."

"A dwarf?" Megdi asked in astonishment.

"Of course it was not an ordinary dwarf," Gurgar said. "It was a *dng,* and the word *dng* came up in the letter again and again. I had to write that word at least fifty times."

"You?" Megdi asked, wondering if he had heard right.

"I was his scribe, you know," the old man said with a sly smile. "Scribe to the great Pharaoh. At that time the southern frontier of Egypt, the granite gate at Aswân, was entrusted to a prince named Herkhuf. This prince was enterprising, brave, fully able to cope with his difficult task. He took it into his head to discover new ways into the interior of Africa. He began an exploration of the land of Iretyet, and returned home laden with treasures after a journey of eight months. On his third exploration he encountered the prince of Yam, who was determined 'to sweep the Libyans before him into the western corner of the sky.' Herkhuf persuaded the forces of Yam and Libya to make peace with one another. In gratitude for his services as a mediator he was given three hundred asses loaded with incense, panther hides, oil, ivory, dice, and other precious articles. And when Herkhuf's caravan set out for home, accompanied by an honour guard provided by the prince of Yam, all the chiefs through whose territory he passed gave the Egyptian their

105

best cattle and showed him the safest way over the mountains of Iretyet. Naturally we in Egypt heard all about it, by word of mouth and by various missives. Pepi I, who was the Pharaoh, praised the lord of the South and received him with date wine, bread, and beer when he came to the court."

"But what has this to do with the dwarf and Pepi II?" Megdi asked in perplexity.

"I was just coming to that," Gurgar assured him. "The dwarf comes in a little later in the story. For Herkhuf was so pleased with the results of his third expedition that he undertook a fourth. Pepi I had died and the child Pepi II now came to the throne. Herkhuf went to the heart of Africa and he was given a dwarf by one of the rulers there. Naturally he no sooner got home than he informed the Pharaoh, Pepi II, of this prize acquisition. He must have known the Pharaoh would be intrigued."

"And was he?" Megdi queried eagerly.

"The Pharaoh sent for me, his scribe, at once," Grugar said, again with that odd, faraway look on his face. "The words he wished me to send to Herkhuf fluttered like birds out of his mouth: 'From the king himself. In the year two on the sixteenth day of the third month of the flood. To Pharaoh's closest friend, Herkhuf, gifted speaker of many languages. My Majesty has learned from your letter that you have returned safely with the troops who accompanied you, and have brought back treasures from Yam. You have written furthermore that you have brought from the land of the spirits a dance-dwarf for the dances of the god, a true *dng* like that *dng* which was brought to Egypt from the incense land of Punt by the treasurer Baverdad under the reign of King Asosi. You have
106

assured my Majesty that the like of this has never been fetched from the land of Yam before, namely, so wonderful a *dng*.

" 'So then my Majesty will heap honours upon you, that you will be resplendent still for your children and grandchildren, and all will say that nothing compares to what my Majesty did for his closest friend Herkhuf when he came down from Yam and brought with him a *dng*. So come at once to court by barge and bring this *dng* with you, whom you have brought alive and well out of the land of spirits. When you are bringing him on the ship, see to it that capable men hold him on both sides, lest he fall into the Nile. And when.

The dwarf Seneb is carried in a litter and honoured

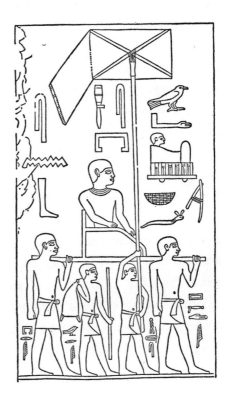

he sleeps at night, let your most faithful men guard his tent, and look to him yourself ten times every night. For my Majesty wishes to see this *dng* more eagerly than all the treasures of the land of mines together with all those of the incense land of Punt. As soon as you appear at the palace, the *dng* living, safe, and sound at your side, my Majesty will do greater things for you than did Pharaoh Asosi for his treasurer Baverdad, for my heart craves nothing more passionately than to see this *dng*. Orders have been issued to all high priests and heads of cities on your way to take good care of you and the *dng* on your voyage.' "

"Dng!" Megdi burst into laughter. "What a funny word."

"I suppose I should have said *deneg*," Gurgar said; his faraway expression had departed and he looked his familiar old self again. "That was how the word was spoken. But at that period only the consonants were written, and since I wrote those three letters over and over again, they have remained that way in my memory."

"Pepi II must have been a king who loved to laugh!" Megdi said.

Gurgar shook his head. "Not at all. He was a sad Pharaoh. Perhaps that was why he wanted the dwarf so badly. He must have had a pretty good sense of the ruin that was threatening Egypt. But he was not the man to head it off. He did his best, though. He issued decree after decree, and a good many of them were excellent decrees. 'My Majesty has commanded that canals, ponds, and sycamores must not be taxed . . .' and so on. But the predecessors of Pepi, the kings of the Sixth Dynasty, had revealed so many weaknesses that the people could no longer believe in their omnipotence. They no longer thought that Pharaoh controlled the stars, the flood of the Nile, and the growth of crops. He was no longer regarded as a god who could strike down rebels with a mere glance.

"Nevertheless, something of the old aura of godhood lingered on, so that the king could be blamed for natural disasters. In famine years the people demanded: Why does he permit the drought? The emaciated figures carved into the stone blocks along the ramp to the pyramid of Unas ask that question. How could an aged king bring about *maat,* the heavenly order, upon earth? How could a man who was incapable of restoring his own youth bring the flush of young growth to the fields of Egypt? The powerful nobles of the court and the provincial administration saw their hour coming. And when the Pharaohs took to having the 'words of the god' chiselled by workmen into the walls of their tombs, the secret texts fell into the hands of unauthorized persons. Such persons thought they possessed magic powers and that special knowledge which could be attained only by passing through the stern ordeals of initiations.

"In the end it was said of these ordinary men: 'There is no longer anything at all that they do not know.' The people rose up to shake off the authority of feeble kings and the exploitation of a

Famine relief from the ramp to the pyramid of Unas

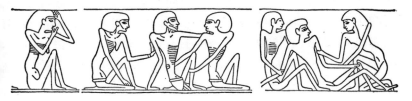

conscienceless nobility. Why should they not take their fate into their own hands, since in the secret doctrines it was said: 'Man's heart is his own god?' The result was a time of terrible troubles."

Gurgar pointed to the remains of Pepi's pyramid. "I saw the beginning of this pyramid," he said. "But I did not see it finished. The building of it and the three small pyramids for the king's wives went on for nearly a hundred years. Within a few hours all was destroyed. A nobleman named Ipuver has described what took place. We still have his account; it has survived the centuries. Horrified by the abysmal misery into which Egypt was being plunged from one day to the next, Ipuver cried out: 'Behold, things have occurred which have not happened since the remotest times. The king has been overthrown by the rebels. Behold, he who was buried as Horus has been snatched from the tomb. The secret of the pyramids has been exposed. The seat of the court has been overturned within an hour. The king's diadem, the holy serpent, has been stolen from its hiding place. The secrets of the two lands have been revealed. But he whose hand now holds the rod of rule wishes to quell the rebellion without violence. Savage slaughter rages in the streets, but the timid ruler cannot take heart and command the destroyers to stop. It is like serving roast meats to the lion, and bringing fodder to the crocodile. People eat grass and rinse it down with water. They rob food from the mouth of the swine, in order not to starve. There are no longer any aristocratic families. Gold is hung round the necks of the maids. The mistresses wail: Give us food to eat! Misery passes through the land; blood is everywhere; violence burns in all hearts. Sailors no longer sail to Byblos
110

to fetch wood for the cedar coffins. Laughter is no more heard. Those who owned clothes now go in rags. Those who looked at their faces in the water now own bronze mirrors. Those who had been powerful lament: Would that I were dead! The children wail: Would that I had never been born! The land turns upon itself like a potter's wheel. Oh, would that God had extinguished man in the seed! But he permitted him to be born. Where is the lord of the universe today? Has he fallen asleep? Was there ever a shepherd who looked on unmoved while his herd died?'

"So did Ipuver bewail the times and its calamities. The kingdom of the Pharaohs had been shaken to its foundations. Tombs and pyramids were broken open, capital cities and palaces levelled, documents burned. Women implored heaven that they might bear no children. Weary of life, people tried to persuade their souls to leave this earth upon which such terrible things were possible. Men were frightened of themselves, and those of good will who did not want to enrich themselves by taking the property of the overthrown mighty ones, desperately looked for something to believe in. They found it nowhere, unless they found it in their own hearts.

"But amid all the horrors of destruction, Ipuver nevertheless had a word of encouragement for those who had lost hope. After all the disorder a new king would appear, he predicted, a king who would be a good shepherd to his people."

"And did such a king come?"

"He did," Gurgar said. "A new family of kings came from the South, and they built their capital on land which they first had to create."

111

Gurgar stood up and looked toward the setting sun. Megdi looked in the same direction, across the desert which seemed to drink up the red pouring down from the crimson sky. Silently, the old man and his young companion descended the slope of the fallen pyramid. Over the desert sands came a breath of cool air. Gurgar and Megdi speeded their steps. Shortly before they reached Mariette's house, the old man said: "One of these new kings, the third Amenemhet, played an important part in my life. When I was your age, his pyramid was opened, and I was the first to enter the innermost chamber, where his sarcophagus stood."

Megdi flung questions at Gurgar. But the old man said only: "Let your father tell you about it. He can also tell you more about the new kings than I can."

Father came along almost at once, and took them back to Cairo. Megdi did not want to ask his father any questions while Gurgar was with them. But as soon as they were alone at home, he asked: "Was Gurgar really the first to reach Amenemhet's sarcophagus?"

"That's something you can check on in books," his father said.

"And he was my age at the time?"

"Certainly he was no bigger than you—otherwise he would not have been able to squeeze through."

"But," Megdi went on hesitantly, "was he also King Pepi's scribe?"

"Gurgar is convinced of that."

Opposite: *Temple of Hatshepsut in Dai al-Bahri. Left, temple of Mentuhotep (Eleventh Dynasty) (above); Der el Medineh, "the hidden city"(below)*

"And are you?"

"All I can say," Father replied, "is that you can learn more about the Old Kingdom from Gurgar than from anyone else. He has told me things that no one could possibly know, and that turned out to be astonishingly true in the light of later finds. Either these things exist in his memory, as he claims, or he can somehow cast his mind perfectly back to an age three thousand years ago. It comes to the same thing, after all."

Opposite: *The great colonnade in the temple area of Karnak*

THE NEW LAND

There was still a week before the promised journey to Upper Egypt, and Megdi went to school as usual. At least the teacher thought he was there, but Megdi knew differently. He took up his pen when all the other boys took up theirs, but what he wrote in his notebook would have thoroughly mystified his teacher. He was drawing hieroglyphics. While the others were listening to explanations of this or that method in arithmetic, Megdi's thoughts were with Cheops or Pepi or Nefertiti, the beautiful queen whose name in hieroglyphics was one of the first he learned to write. He was collecting hieroglyphics with the same enthusiasm that some boys collect stamps. Each new one that he mastered gave him additional pleasure. When Father tested him for the first time toward the end of the week, Megdi could already read and write twenty Pharaohs' names.

Father went to the cupboard where he kept his treasures, opened a drawer, and took out a plain-looking scarab. The smooth underside was engraved with hieroglyphics, surrounded by a ring: a royal name.

"Tut-ankh-amen," Megdi deciphered.

Father smiled. "Very good," he said. "And now keep the scarab for luck. You'll want it along on this little jaunt of ours." Megdi flushed with pleasure.

"Could you tell me something, Father, about the king whose sarcophagus Gurgar discovered?" he reminded his father.

Father spread a map on the table and pointed to a green spot. "Right here," he said, "on the edge of Faiyum, the new kings built a great storage dam which made this area one of the most fruitful districts in Egypt. New and better times began for the whole country when the first Amenemhet came out of the South. He had risen from vizier to Pharaoh. 'Shining like the sun, he marched through the two lands to annihilate injustice. He taught each city to renew its boundaries on the others, and he set up their boundary stones as firm as heaven itself, because he loved the truth.' So the ancient accounts tell us. This Pharaoh inaugurated the Twelfth Dynasty which brought the Middle Kingdom to the height of its glory. The new rulers had more difficulties to contend with than the older Pharaohs. They were new kings, of a disputed line, and they had to uphold their power amidst conspiracies and attempted assassination. Their faces are stamped with the determination to clear up the chaos that their predecessors had left behind. These were brave rulers, and they encouraged the people to believe that they could surmount all the difficulties of the country. They gathered in the strayed herd, as Ipuver had prophesied.

"The kings of the Twelfth Dynasty succeeded in reuniting Egypt and in securing her borders. These Pharaohs had their statues placed not only in their tombs, but on the frontiers of the land as well.

"One of these kings, Sesostris, became the model for the Egyp-

tians; he was regarded as the most clearheaded and benevolent o
all rulers. Even the Greeks borrowed this tradition. Sesostris coul
truly say of himself: 'I have taken this land upon my shoulders.
Ages later the story was told that when after thirty-three years o
rule his eyesight began to fade, he turned the throne over to hi
heirs. This came to be a noble precedent. Almost all the Pharaoh
of this great dynasty divided their power with their successors a
soon as they no longer felt able to sustain the tasks of ruling.

"Under these kings Egypt celebrated the *hebsed,* the festival o
renewal. Egypt had gone down to destruction—and now Egyp
was stronger and more vital than ever. Death had lost its sting, fo
the nation and for the individual. During the time of troubles ;
poet had asked:

> To whom shall I speak today?
> The faces are turned away.
> Each holds his head lowered, looking not on his brother.
> Death comes upon me like the fragrance of myrrh
> When one sits under the awning on a wind-cooled day.
> Death comes to me like the perfume of the lotus
> When one sits drunk from celebrating by the water.
> Death stands before me like the dawn in the sky,
> Like the dawning of knowledge, when one understood not.

But now the poets proclaimed that man could not be conquered i
he refused to give up. The central figures of the two most importan
novels of the Middle Kingdom are men who face their destiny un
afraid."

"Novels?" Megdi asked in surprise.

"Yes, we can call them novels, though they were not exactly that," Father said. "Still, they were lively stories about real people and real conditions. I am thinking of the Story of Sinuhe, the Egyptian, and the Story of the Man from the Salt Field."

Father took down a book from his crowded book-shelves and leafed through it until he had found what he was seeking. The pages were covered with hieroglyphics. But Father seemed to know the story almost by heart, for he only glanced at the symbols now and then as he spoke:

"A man from the salt field who had a large family looked one day into his grain chests and saw that the bottom was barely covered. So he loaded up his six or seven donkeys and set off for Faiyum, intending to exchange salt and products of his workmanship for food supplies. On the way he passed by the estate of Renzi, the Lord High Chamberlain. Or rather, he did not get quite that far. For a certain Thutnakht, a lower official who was steward of the estate, saw the man from the salt field coming with his donkeys. He saw, and made his decision. Hastily, he had linen spread across the road. To the left of the road was a wheat field, to the right a canal. The man from the salt field came 'on the road which belongs to all,' led his donkeys as far as the estate, saw the linen, and hesitated. He was a man who did not wish to harm anyone, and he was loath to tear or dirty the linen of a high official. But how was he to go on? A canal is no road for a donkey. In the field the grain stood high. Finally the man tried leading each donkey in turn carefully through the rows of wheat. And then what the cunning Thutnakht had expected happened: a donkey plucked a mouthful of wheat.

117

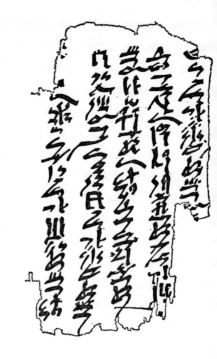

Hieratic script of the Middle Kingdom (from the story of the Man from the Salt Field): "This Thutnakht said: 'Be still, you peasant! Are you trampling on my linen?' The peasant said: 'I do so that you may praise me. My way is right. . . .'"

Instantly the steward, who had lain in ambush, descended upon the poor man. 'Donkeys who unlawfully snatch the Lord High Chamberlain's wheat belong to him!' he cried.

"The man from the salt field apologized in touching words. Politely, but without bending his back, he defended his donkeys. The steward, however, called his men and they drove the little caravan with its whole load into the farmyard. Then the peasant flared up: 'The road belongs to me as well as to you! You blocked it. I wanted to spare what belonged to you. You led the donkeys into temptation. And now you lay hand upon them because one of them took a mouthful of wheat. I know the master of this estate, Lord Cham-

118

berlain Renzi. He is a man who drives away the robbers. He will not tolerate robbers on his own estate.'

"The steward broke off a tamarisk branch and gave his reply with that until the man from the salt field lay on the ground. But in spite of the beating he refused to give way. For four days he laid siege to the estate. He did not see his donkeys again, and was mocked for his pains. Then he set out to find Lord Chamberlain Renzi. Just as the Lord Chamberlain was about to enter his official barge, the peasant came before him and described the injustice he had endured. He did so in such well-chosen words that the Lord Chamberlain listened, and deigned to question the lower officials who accompanied him about the matter. These officials instantly took the side of the steward, who was one of their own. 'Surely this peasant has not paid his taxes, or has done so to the wrong official. Would our capable Thutnakht go through such a business over a little salt? If the man continues to fuss, no doubt he will return the salt. . . .'

"Such were the opinions of the subordinates. Not a word was said about the donkeys, or about the peasant's starving family. Bitterness filled the heart of the peasant, but he said nothing in order not to disturb the thoughts of the Lord Chamberlain, who stood attentively listening to the argument of the others. Finally the Lord beckoned to the peasant. The peasant stepped forward and spoke of the high opinion he had of the Lord Chamberlain: 'The Nile will be happy to bear your barge, for you are kind, a brother to the deserted soul, free of covetousness, a great one who will answer the cry for help from my lips. Behold me! What belongs to me has been taken from me, and injustice heaped upon me!'

"Astonished, Renzi listened. The words of the man from the salt field touched him. He promised to help, and when he came to the king his first words were: 'My lord and master, I have found a peasant who can speak as I have heard none speak before.'

"Then the king sent for the peasant, gave him gifts, sent provisions to his starving family, and had his scribe write down every word spoken by the man from the salt field. But the peasant refused to forget the wrong which had been done him. Justice, *maat*, had been violated. He demanded atonement. Fearlessly, he addressed his questions to Renzi: 'Are you not like the Nile who revives the parched fields? Would you become a destroying torrent of water for the man who seeks justice? Is the balance ever mistaken? You and the balance are one; your tongue is the tongue of the balance, your heart its weight, your lips its beam.'

"But the Lord Chamberlain was not inclined to pass judgement against Thutnakht. The peasant could no longer contain his indignation. He criticized Renzi. That was too much for the high official. He made two of his servants give the man a sound thrashing. Yet the man from the salt field remained intransigent as ever. 'You make common cause with the robber,' he cried to Renzi, 'you who ought to be the dike shielding the poor. Instead you are the raging torrent which covers the property of the poor man with wickedness. It is your office to be like clothing, so that no man may freeze; like the peaceful sky after storms; like water that quenches thirst. He whose sail is made of lies will never reach land.'

"Renzi did not reply. Then the man from the salt field declared that he would appeal to Anubis. That was the same as saying that

120

he would take his own life because he did not wish to remain any longer in a world without justice. And at that point Renzi yielded. He went to the king with all the laments of the eloquent peasant, and the Pharaoh took more delight in this than in anything else he had known in his country."

Father looked up from the book. "The end of the story has been lost," he said. "But there can scarcely be any doubt that the donkeys were restored to the persistent plaintiff, and that the thief was punished, and so a complete victory for *maat*, for the heavenly order on earth, was won because the man was courageous and enduring."

"I like that man from the salt field," Megdi said. "He had a lot of courage. Can I hear the other story, the one about Sinuhe the Egyptian?"

"He, too, lived thirty-five hundred years ago," Father said, as he leafed through the book for the story. "But unlike the man from the salt field, Sinuhe was an aristocrat who belonged to the court. His adventure began in the thirtieth year of the reign of Amenemhet I. Sinuhe was accompanying Amenemhet's son Sesostris, the heir to the throne, on a campaign against the Libyans. Just after the enemy had been defeated and his herds captured as booty, word reached the army that the Pharaoh had 'risen to Heaven and united with the Sun.' The capital was paralyzed, the message said.

"We know little about the political manoeuvrings that led to the behaviour of the characters in this story. At any rate, Sesostris secretly slipped away from the army, we are told, and Sinuhe was so terrified that he hid. Apparently Sinuhe feared uprisings in the capital, and thought that he would be held responsible, for he fled to

121

the delta. Near the quarries of the Red Mountain he crossed the Nile, moving by night until he reached the wall that the Pharaohs had erected to protect Egypt from the Bedouins, crossed it, and fled on as far as the Bitter Lakes. In the desert he was without water. His throat burned, he fell down in the sand, and suddenly the thought came into his mind: This is the taste of death. A passing band of Bedouins came to his rescue. He was passed from one country to the next. Finally he came to the prince of Retenu, who took him in, gave him his daughter to wife, allowed him to choose a province to rule over. Sinuhe chose the land of Yaa. There were figs and wine, honey and oil, barley and wheat, cattle and sheep. Sinuhe lived well. His children grew up. He gave shelter to travellers, avenged the victims of robbery, and drove intruders from the prince's pastures and walls. And the prince placed him at the head of all his children.

"Then envious souls raised their heads; they sent forth a man of gigantic proportions who challenged Sinuhe to battle. The Egyptian said to the prince of Retenu: 'I am a foreigner who is not loved; but if there is a bull who wishes to fight, I shall also be a bull, and fight.' And Sinuhe stretched his bow and prepared his arrows and axe. The hearts of the people of Retenu burned for him. The giant attacked. But Sinuhe drove him back, and when the Asiatic took flight, an arrow struck him in the back of the neck. He cried out and fell on his face. Then Sinuhe swung his axe and drove it into the giant as if he were a tree. All the Asiatics who were watching shouted in agony.

"Now Sinuhe felt certain that the Pharaoh whom he had secretly deserted had strengthened his arm and allowed him to fell he strong man. 'For he has rejuvenated my body!' he cried aloud. And he will have the mercy to call me home to the land of my fahers!'

"And that is what happened. Sesostris sent for Sinuhe to come 1ome, so that he would have his eternal house in Egypt and not n a foreign land, where the dead were only wrapped in a sheep-kin. Sinuhe gave his property to his children, whom he left be-1ind. In solemn ceremony, he was taken back to Egypt and led to the palace. When he beheld Pharaoh, he fell to the ground. His heart was no longer in his body. He did not know whether he was living or dead. The king's children were frightened of the stranger. But His Majesty raised him up among his councillors. He was taken to a bath, given precious garments, rubbed with myrrh and fine oil. His hair was shorn and combed; the years vanished from his body. All the dirt he had brought back with him was cast out into the desert. Pharaoh had a pretty house of wood built for him, and what was far more important, a stone house for the life after death. All the work was entrusted to the king's own craftsmen. Moreover, the king honoured Sinuhe the Egyptian, who had become an Asiatic and then an Egyptian once more, who had overcome the desert and the giant in the land of Retenu—by giving him a statue coated with gold.

"Like the man from the salt field, Sinuhe had mastered his destiny. Here were two characters who, in situations that appeared hopeless, proved their worth. These stories of the Middle Kingdom illustrate a principle which, apparently, the Egyptians held as dear as we do: that in the end what really counts is to endure and triumph over the blows of destiny."

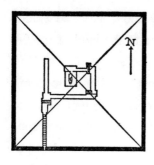

Outline of the pyramid of Hawara

Father closed the book. "I promised to tell you the story of Gurgar's great discovery," he said. "Perhaps it is not quite as great a feat as he likes to make it out. Petrie was really responsible for it all, for Gurgar was only a boy. Nevertheless, he certainly played a part in the discovery, just because he was still a boy. It's natural that he should remember it as his great triumph.

"Petrie, who, you will remember, was the first man to measure precisely the great pyramids, had come across the modest pyramids on the outskirts of Faiyum which the kings of the Twelfth Dynasty had built out of mud bricks. These pyramids had long since been stripped of their stone outer coating. To the fore of one lay a huge mass of ruins which had once been a palace for the dead, with a bewildering array of corridors and chambers which the Greeks called a labyrinth. Petrie could find not the slightest clue to the owner of this shapeless mound which had once been a pyramid. He decided to break into the mound. In all the pyramids that Petrie had investigated up to that time, the entrance had been on the northern side. Petrie hunted in vain on that side. Neither was there any opening to the east. Finally Petrie began driving a shaft diagonally through the pyramid. The walls he attacked were made of crumbly stuff; he had to dig for weeks before he reached a hard core. The shaft was a black infernal pit into which he and his few helpers ventured daily in fear of their lives. Their tools were wretched; everything had to be done by hand. The workers grumbled, threatened to quit. But Petrie refused to give up. At last he penetrated to a chamber made of stone. He pried one block loose. The glow of his torch fell upon two sarcophagi. Both had been broken open. Grave robbers had done thorough work a few thousand years ago. Nevertheless, Petrie tried to squeeze through the opening. He could not. Then he called the boy who had stuck at his side all through the trying excavation; he tied a rope around Gurgar's waist and handed him a candle. Gurgar slid through the aperture. Held securely by the rope, he was lowered into the chamber. His feet found support only after he was already up to his waist in ground water and mud. He splashed around the sarcophagi, but found nothing to indicate whose mummies had been placed in them. Then he began poking about in the mud. At last he came upon an alabaster vessel. He handed it up to Petrie—and heard the archaeologist give an exclamation of joy. 'Amenemhet!' Petrie said. The king's name was inscribed on the vessel that Gurgar had found.

"After that the opening was widened and Petrie himself climbed down into the chamber. He found sacrificial gifts, all dedicated to Princess Ptahnofru. Obviously the second sarcophagus had been intended for her.

"Still Petrie was not satisfied. He wanted to find the entrance to the pyramid, and to discover how the grave robbers had broken in.

For weeks he dug his way through muddy, rubble-choked passages Gurgar followed him like a shadow. Through gravel and crumbled mud bricks they worked their way toward the exit. Contrary to all previous experience, it was on the south side. Petrie pondered this riddle. How had the robbers been able to find it? How had they succeeded in making their way to the burial chamber in spite of all obstacles? The passage from the entrance led down a staircase into an empty room. But appearances were deceptive. The roof of this lower room was a tremendous trap door. If one could lift it or break through, one would be able to advance a good deal closer to the burial chamber. The robbers, it was plain, had succeeded in doing so, and had even found their way into a corridor sealed by blocks of stone.

"Having discovered their trail, Petrie reasoned out the rest of the story like a detective. Such a crime required not only extraordinary intelligence, but weeks of wearing toil. How could robbers have carried out such weeks of work in an area which, beyond a doubt, was guarded every moment of the day and night? There was only one explanation: the guards must have been accomplices of the

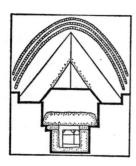

*Section through the burial chamber of
Amenemhet III in the pyramid of Hawara*

robbers, must have told them where the pyramid could be entered, and how to proceed from obstacle to obstacle.

"Petrie felt better then. His toil, trouble, risk, had not been for nothing. The empty sarcophagi were no longer such a disappointment. The pillagers had taken all the treasures, but there was still something left for the scientists—another piece of knowledge. As for the boy who had so willingly and ably helped in that crucial moment, he became even more closely united to the scientist now by this new bond. Wherever the archaeologist went, his young helper was by his side, eager to assist and learn.

"From that time on," Father continued, "Gurgar was not just a boy casually hired when another hand was needed for an excavation. He was someone special and a highly prized member of any excavation team. It is surprising how important it is to have such people in your expedition. Their influence on the ordinary workmen is incalculable. Every reis, the foreman who digs with the archaeologists, is a man who has not only a lot of experience but a high sense of principle. Incidentally, Hofni, who is off with Ghoneim helping to excavate the forgotten pyramid, was another of the boys who attached himself to Petrie's team. He also took part in the excavation of the Amenemhet pyramid. He was quite alone when, scratching through the crumbled bricks, he came upon a princess's diadem. It was a uraeus snake of pure gold, inlaid with lapis lazuli, garnets, cornelian, and turquoise. He could have hidden it somewhere and sold it on the sly; it would have brought him more wealth than a lifetime of hard work brings to a fellah. But it did not even occur to Hofni to do that. Breathlessly, he ran to Petrie with his find, his face radiant with triumph. . . . That

127

is how Gurgar would like all Egyptians to be," Father concluded. "For thirty years he has been trying in vain to make honest men out of those crafty Qurnese. Now he has placed his hopes upon you attaching one of the boys 'to the rope.' "

"The chances are pretty slim, aren't they?" Megdi said.

Father pointed to the scarab of Tutankhamen, which Megdi still clutched in his hand. "Believe in your good-luck charm," he said encouragingly. "And who knows, it may work out. By the way, you will want to put your scarab in a leather purse and wear it around your neck. But now it's time to get to bed. Tomorrow at this time, we'll be beginning our journey."

Megdi slept poorly that night. And the following night, too, on the train to Luxor, his sleep was troubled by wild dreams.

Opposite: *Fellahin threshing and winnowing* (above); *View from the Faiyum toward the pyramid of Illahun* (below)

THE OLD VILLAGE

Megdi was standing at the window when the train pulled into the station in Luxor. The rising sun had already placed a fiery comb upon the horizon, and the wings of the hawks that circled the railroad station shot crimson sparks.

A friendly Nubian wearing a white *galabia* and white headband was waiting for Father, Megdi, and Gurgar at the wheel of a shining new Ford. He had been sent by the director of the excavations at Qurna. Father was supposed to inspect those excavations. That was what he was here for. As far as anyone knew, Megdi and Gurgar were along just for company.

"Let us get across the river as quickly as possible," Father said to the driver. It was well to have some headstart on the swarms of tourists who day after day pour noisily out of the hotels into the sailboats, cross the Nile in the morning breeze, pile into the smelly old jalopies which serve for taxis, are driven to the three usual tombs, the usual restaurant, and the two usual temples, and

Opposite: *The colossi of Memnon (statues of Amenophis III) in western Thebes* (above); *Courtyard of a dwelling in Qurna* (below)

then return across the Nile in the same boats toward six o'clock in the evening, to go back to their various hotels.

On the short ride down to the Nile, Megdi saw with amazement that the left side of the road was lined with shops and houses, while on the right stood ancient pylons and the remains of temple walls. Over all this towered a hill crowned by a mosque. Old and new were crowded together side by side on this soil where hundred-gated Thebes had once stood. An asphalt road wound around the fallen temple of the god Amen, and above the rows of pillars, the muezzin's call to prayers sounded from the minaret.

"Can't we look at the temple while we're here?" Megdi begged.

"In three or four days," Father put him off. "We'll also be going to Karnak, the most impressive temple area in all of Egypt. Karnak was the sacred heart of the New Kingdom. But now we want to pay our visit to the good people of Qurna." He pointed across the Nile.

"Fine people to visit! Robbers and counterfeiters!" the old man muttered.

They drove a short distance along the shore road. Beyond the strip of green river valley on the other shore, Megdi saw a chain of ridges, crowned by a peak of bare rock which formed a natural pyramid.

"El Qurn, the seat of the goddess who loves silence," Father said. "Beyond lies the Valley of the Kings."

At the landing place where the excavators kept their boat, a second Nubian, as competent and attentive as the driver of their car, took over the guests and their baggage. A good wind puffed the sail of the tall-masted *ayasa,* and they moved swiftly toward the opposite shore. The Nubian sang softly under his breath.

Beyond the landing stage Megdi caught sight of the jalopies his father had mentioned: row upon row of cars that seemed to have escaped from some automobile graveyard. There was also a squad of donkeys equipped with dilapidated saddles, and a number of bicycles. One of the bicycles was brand-new, though not destined to remain new long, for its proud and eager owner had pushed it so far forward that the front wheel rested in the Nile. The crowd of jabbering dragomans did not so much as waste a glance on the three men and the boy who stepped off the excavators' boat.

"All scoundrels!" Gurgar declared. "Scoundrels with smiling faces. All they think about morning, noon, and night is how to extract money from the tourists, and gold from the tombs. Hopeless cases as far as we are concerned." He pointed to the new bicycle. "That was never paid for," he said contemptuously. "I'll wager it was swapped for the left foot of Ramses II. Or to be more exact, for one of the fifteen hundred forged left feet of Ramses that this fellow has thrown on the market."

"Don't exaggerate," Father put in. "I dare say he hasn't sold as many as thirteen hundred."

The Nubian tied up the boat, carried their baggage from the *ayasa* to a jeep, and they started off at a leisurely speed toward Qurna. The road was good, lined on both sides by canals and thriving fields. They had gone about half the distance when they came to a table standing by the road, behind which sat a man in uniform who was noting down the licence number of every car that went by. A short distance away, a new village began.

"What good is it just to note licence numbers?" Gurgar grumbled. "He ought to be searching every car."

When they reached the new village in Qurna, Gurgar took Megdi on a brief tour. The place looked as if it had only a moment before fallen out of the cloudless sky, or sprung up from the pleasant green fields all around. The houses had attractive doorways and light-coloured walls that promised coolness; they were neat, inviting—and all but a few were empty.

"These buildings were planned by one of Egypt's foremost architects. They were built as a gift from the government to the people of Qurna. And the people don't want them! Can you understand that?"

They drove on. It was only about two miles farther to old Qurna. In the open fields, just a stone's throw from the edge of the village, two colossal stone statues guarded the way: cracked giants upon cracked thrones. The heads had weathered beyond the point of recognition.

"Both of them represent the same Pharaoh," Father declared. "Amenophis III. These statues are all that remain of the tremendous mortuary temple that this Pharaoh had erected here, together with a palace and artificial lake in which he and his queen went pleasure-sailing in a gold-studded barge. The Greeks thought one of these huge statues was that of King Memnon. When the sun rose a mysterious sound came from the colossus—they called it Memnon's lament. It was heard no more after a Roman emperor had the cracks in the granite repaired."

Megdi stood looking up at the stone giants. Suddenly Gurgar threw his hands into the air and uttered a piercing cry. A swarm of pigeons fluttered up from the heads of the statues, and Megdi saw plainly the traces they had left behind.

132

"Typical Qurnese!" Gurgar railed. "They respect nothing." He glared in the direction of the village—looking for the moment like a hawk about to descend upon its prey. "There they are, huddling in their caves," he said grimly. "Jackals, each and every one of them. . . . Look over there," he urged Megdi, "and tell me whether that is a decent place for living human beings!"

It was the strangest village that Megdi had ever seen: hundreds of dark rectangles cut into the cliff which rose out of the desert toward the west. There were a few houses—square, unadorned boxes; but most of the people seemed to live right in the cliff. There was not a tree anywhere in the village. Black doorways, sand, stone: that was all. "It is like the end of the world," Megdi thought.

"And yet they could live in that model village you've just seen," Gurgar groaned. "Built especially for them. They don't deserve it —they don't deserve anything."

"Lucky they can't hear you," Megdi's father commented. "They'd enjoy a good laugh."

"They have been laughing at me for years," Gurgar replied.

Father would not grant this. "No, they do not laugh at you. They really envy you. Idolize you, in fact."

"But why?" the old man said with some heat. "Because I have found more gold than all of them put together! Actually they think me a fool because I kept none of it for myself." He waved his hand violently through the air, as though to wipe out a distasteful vision. "Robbers and forgers, every single one of them. I give up, as far as they are concerned. But perhaps there is still hope for some of the boys. Perhaps. That depends on you," he added with a glance at Megdi.

133

They drove to a roomy house on the east side of Qurna. It was known as James Henry Breasted's house, for the great American historian had lived there for several years. Now it belonged to Sheik Ali.

"The grandson of a robber chief!" Gurgar whispered to Megdi as the sheik loomed up in the doorway: an extremely tall man with bushy eyebrows over deep-sunk eyes. He greeted the archaeologist and Gurgar with effusive courtesy, then drew Megdi into his arms. "Your father and Ali: friends for more years than a man has fingers. Gurgar and Ali: friends for more years than we four men have fingers. You are a man by now, aren't you?" he asked Megdi, and laughed with flashing teeth.

With the graciousness of a prince he led his guests into the courtyard, one half of which was green, the other half yellow. The borderline between desert and grassland ran right through the middle of the yard and house. The sheik clapped his hands. Two servants appeared. The sheik called out a few words to them, and they vanished again. Sheik Ali then led his guests to a table in the shade of a group of palms. At a wave of his hand, breakfast was served. It was like coming to the house of a magician. While they ate and drank, Sheik Ali joked and told stories.

There seemed to be a second house attached to the main house. It looked like a fort, bristling with rifle barrels and the mouths of cannon. On closer inspection Megdi saw that the dangerous-looking spikes were only dry tree branches. Pigeons were roosting on these branches, and other pigeons were going in and out of the "cannon," which, Megdi realized, were only a great many round openings in a gigantic dovecot. The sheik led his guests up the steps between the house and the dovecot into the upper story, and
134

opened three doors. Here were the rooms in which Megdi, his father, and Gurgar were to stay.

"I like Sheik Ali," Megdi said a little later, when he was standing with Gurgar on the landing of the staircase, looking out at the colossi.

"He's another great rascal," Gurgar murmured obsessively.

"But he's Father's friend, and your friend, too," Megdi protested.

"And the grandson of the worst grave robber in all Egypt. A complete scoundrel," the old man repeated. "Just like all those others who lie in wait by the Nile for tourists, or produce *ushabtis* and heads of Nefertiti out of thin air."

Megdi glanced uncertainly at Gurgar; he was not sure how he was to take this. Now the old man pointed over the wall, and Megdi saw in the midst of the fields a sakieh (water wheel) being driven by a donkey. Round and round the donkey trotted, and now, as Megdi listened, he heard the grinding of gears and saw the buckets rise up out of the well, tip over, and pour water into a channel. A village girl was sitting on the crude seat between the shafts. Nearby stood a lazy-looking camel; two boys sat cross-legged beside it.

"Achmed and Jacob," Gurgar whispered. "They are just about your age. Their fathers are the busiest counterfeiters in the village."

"Do you know them, then?" Megdi asked in surprise.

"I know all of them."

"Who is the girl?"

"Titi," Gurgar said. "She is Achmed's sister. Not important for us. The girls are kept pretty busy with house and field work. But Achmed and Jacob are important for us. They have plenty of time, and some day they will be men who have a say in this village."

135

Megdi saw that the two boys were playing some kind of board game. "I'd like to go over and meet them," he said.

"Later," Gurgar decided. "First I want to show you where the boys live. That is something you really have to see."

Once out of their host's compound, Gurgar and Megdi made their way through the hot sand, past neglected water wheels, up to the dwellings of the "counterfeiters." Megdi was amazed to see how much life and motion there was on this slope, which from a distance looked dead and deserted. The place was a medley of donkeys, sheep, chickens, camels, women, and children: the air resounded with strident voices and animal noises, and reeked of biting smoke, garlic, and mutton fat, camel dung and spices—a cauldron of seething, turbulent life. The menfolk sat in front of their doors with jugs of water beside them. They were busy with various crafts. They called out lively greetings to Gurgar. He seemed quite a welcome visitor to this community.

Achmed's father was at home, working in his courtyard. He dropped his tools at once and rushed to greet Gurgar and Megdi with a great show of emotion. He ordered his wife to bring coffee, and set out mats for the guests. Beside his basket of tools stood an alabaster vessel.

"Eighteenth Dynasty," he announced proudly, and picked up the simple drill to show Megdi how he went about hollowing the half-finished vase. It was plain that he thought there was nothing wrong in thus increasing the supply of vases from the "Eighteenth Dynasty."

"Here is where Achmed sleeps, and Titi here," Gurgar whis-

136

pered to Megdi, indicating two small structures built up out of mud bricks, with two rows of tiny windows in them. These curious "beds" stood in the courtyard, under the open sky, with sheep and chickens wandering around between them.

After the guests had sipped their coffee, Megdi had a chance to see the interior of the "house." It was a series of inhospitable vaults cut into the cliff, the walls blackened by smoke. There were no tables or chairs, in fact no furniture at all except for a wooden bed, a kerosene stove, two chests, and a number of boxes.

Gurgar was not allowed to leave until he had promised that he would come again next day. The people here were genuinely friendly, Megdi thought, and not at all as he had imagined them. Why had Gurgar fussed and fretted so about this village?

"We won't bother visiting Jacob's home," Gurgar declared. "The set-up is just the same, and the rascals take the same delight in mocking at us and wasting our precious time."

They went on through the village. The dwellings were much like the one they had visited. Everywhere there was squalor and hubbub, the same sharp smells of animals and human beings living together on almost equal terms.

"And now I want you to see what these caves were once like," the old man said. They went on climbing the terraced hillside, and came to a low wall which was obviously fairly new. It enclosed a courtyard similar to all the others which had teemed with ragged small children, chickens, and sheep. The same sort of door was cut into the wall of the cliff, only this one was closed by an iron gate and guarded by a gaffer. The gaffer came forward to greet Gurgar and

Fig harvest with monkeys (*Old Kingdom*)

unlock the gate for them. Inside, a wall suddenly blazed with light. The gaffer had set up a mirror at the entrance so that it threw a broad band of light into the chamber.

There, in lovely colours, fresh, vivid, harmonious, were pictures of life in ancient Egypt. There were two boats in each of which stood a tall man; one man was hurling throwing-sticks at a swarm of brightly plumaged birds, while the other was harpooning fish. Both unmistakably represented the same man. The somewhat smaller wife and the much smaller daughters and servants were also duplicated in both boats. In both paintings the wife anxiously held her husband so that he would not lose his balance, and daughters and servants took charge of the catch which had been fished out of the Nile. Above the waves that swarmed with fish was painted a mass of papyrus reeds crowded with fluttering birds. Obviously, the place was a paradise for fishing and hunting. On another wall, a feast was in progress: the guests in jewelled collars

138

and garments of diaphanous weave were sitting at tables, being entertained by dancing girls and musicians. The elegance and festivity of the occasion was as clear now as when the picture had been painted.

In the next chamber there were pictures of rural life, of pasturing cattle and animals of the desert: a giraffe with a monkey scrambling up its neck as if it were the trunk of a palm tree, leopards, gazelles, and horses, who, with proud manes and prancing gait, drew delicate chariots. Other paintings showed men at work harvesting and treading out grapes, cutting and winnowing grain. Megdi saw a cat with arched back, its claws and teeth sunk into a fish that had fallen from a table. . . . Wall after wall, wherever Megdi looked, glowed with magnificent, colourful life.

"Then that is what is in the caves!" he breathed.

"That used to be !" Gurgar corrected him. "These rooms might easily look just like the ones you saw down there."

"You mean all the caves had paintings like these?"

"Yes, those hovels used to be like this," Gurgar said. "But now,

Trampling and picking grapes (*New Kingdom*)

of course, the process of destruction has gone too far. This one is preserved because no one has moved in. We hope that there are others like it. In fact, we know that there are others like it. The villagers know it too."

"And that's why they're so stubborn," Megdi said.

"Yes, they're hanging on, in hopes of finding treasures. Do you know what is the chief employment of the men in the village? It's digging. They are digging all the time."

"But don't they know—it's against the law!" Megdi protested.

"They don't care about the law."

"Don't these paintings mean anything to them?"

"No indeed," Gurgar declared. "And woe to the tomb that they come across before the archaeologists. They chisel the paintings off the walls piece by piece."

Megdi pointed to a figure whose face was missing. "Was that something they did?"

Gurgar shook his head. "No, that was done several thousand years ago. Whoever did it knew the man who was buried here, and hated him. Since he could not harm him as long as he held office and power, he tried to take his life here in the tomb."

"But the man was already dead," Megdi said, perplexed.

"The enemy wanted to take away his life in the hereafter," Gurgar said. "The life after death, which the ancient Egyptians valued so highly. A man who lost his face or name was dead for good and all. The man who chipped away that face was a belated murderer. He thought he was doing something very terrible. But these villagers take over the caves and destroy the pictures down to
140

the last inch, and don't even know or care what they are doing."

"I'll bring Achmed and Jacob here," Megdi said resolutely. "When they see these paintings, they'll understand."

"If you could do that," Gurgar said, "it would be a good beginning."

Half an hour later Megdi was down in the level fields again, sauntering towards the water wheel. The camel was hitched to the mechanism now, and the donkey was resting in the shade. But the girl still sat on the seat across the shafts, and Achmed and Jacob were still at their game. They did not look up until Megdi's shadow fell across the board. The water wheel stopped turning. Titi was watching.

"Who are you?" Achmed asked sharply.

"Megdi."

"And where do you come from?"

"From there." Megdi pointed to Sheik Ali's house.

Achmed examined Megdi from top to toe. Megdi was wearing shoes, a pair of shorts, and a shirt.

"He dresses like a foreigner," Jacob said to Achmed.

"I come from Cairo," Megdi said.

"Hm, a tourist," Achmed said to Jacob in a condescending tone. "Another tourist, come to look at the same old stuff."

"I've come with Gurgar."

Achmed sniggered. "The excavator who digs for others!"

"My father is an excavator, too," Megdi said in a bold tone. With these boys, obviously, boldness was necessary.

"Too bad," Achmed said.

There was a short silence.

"Could I . . ." Megdi hesitated. "Could I have a game with you?"

"What kind of player are you?" Achmed challenged in a lordly tone. "You're just a Cairo boy. Can you ride a camel? Pick up a snake before it bites you? Tell whether a scorpion is under a stone by just looking at it?"

"Who cares about scorpions, anyway?" Megdi countered. "That's stupid, to think about nothing but camels and scorpions."

There was a tense pause. Finally Achmed started to set up the pieces on the board.

"You will lose," Achmed warned him. "But you can try, if you like."

The sakieh began to turn again. They began the game. Megdi played Achmed, and lost. He then played Jacob. Each time he lost.

"You still won't give up?" Achmed asked after the sixth game.

"No," Megdi said.

"You haven't played this game much, have you? We play it all the time." Achmed eyed Megdi's small body calculatingly. "Bet you're not very strong either."

"What do you mean by that?" Megdi demanded angrily.

"Let's see which of us is stronger."

Megdi stood up at once.

"Let me try him," Jacob offered.

Jacob and Megdi wrestled until Jacob lost his footing.

"You're stronger than you look," Achmed conceded. "Do you want to try me now?"

"Why not?"

The sakieh had stopped again. Achmed stood still and waited for Megdi to make the first lunge. For a long time neither boy could throw the other. Finally both toppled simultaneously to the ground and rolled into the track that the camel and donkey had worn in the mud. The camel looked haughtily down at the two boys who rolled and twisted and gasped until *galabia* and shirt and shorts and faces were all equally smeared with mud. Panting, the boys rose to their feet at last, utterly exhausted; neither had the energy to attack again. Achmed's *galabia* and Megdi's shirt were wide open, and their throats and chests were as dirty as their faces. Suddenly Achmed's hand flew to his chest, and he gave an exclamation of alarm. He began to search in the trampled ground and at last picked up a tiny leather purse with a torn cord. He brushed and blew the dirt carefully away and looked inside.

"Give that to me!" Megdi demanded. "It's mine."

"Yours?" Achmed asked threateningly. "If it's yours, tell me what's in it."

At this moment Titi jumped down from her seat on the shafts and picked up a second little leather purse, just as dirty as the other.

"This one is yours," she said to Achmed.

Achmed looked into it. "Right," he said.

But Megdi had seen that there was a scarab inside. "No, that one must be mine," he said.

Achmed flushed with fury. "What do you mean, that one must be yours! What are the marks on yours?"

With his hand Megdi smoothed a patch of earth. With his finger he traced the hieroglyphic he knew so well in the dust. Achmed examined the drawing carefully. "That's just the mark there is on mine," he said in surprise. Suddenly he looked at Megdi with a different expression in his eyes. "We both have the same scarab."

"Let's see," Jacob said eagerly.

The two scarabs were passed from hand to hand several times. Everyone had to see them both singly and together, to verify the astounding fact that they were really alike. The purses were left lying on the ground while the scarabs were examined, so that in the end it became impossible to decide which scarab belonged to Achmed and which to Megdi.

"It is a sign that we ought to be friends," Achmed said gravely. "We had the same scarab and did not know it."

"Which one do you want?" Megdi asked, embarrassed.

"It doesn't matter," Achmed said. He held out his hand to Megdi, who took one at random. Both boys packed their scarabs into their little leather bags. Megdi felt as if he were receiving it anew as a gift. They all sat down, and Titi started the sakieh again.

"We saw you when you first came," Achmed now admitted. "But we didn't like you because you came in the excavators' car."

"What do you have against the excavators?" Megdi inquired.

"They're nothing but a bunch of robbers," Achmed said. "They take away the things that belong to us. The tombs of Qurna are ours."

"Yours?"

"Of course," Achmed said. "We made them."

"You?"

"It was our ancestors, I mean," Achmed explained. "But we're

Opposite: *View from Qurna across the Theban valley* (above); *Sakieh (water wheels) driven by donkeys, oxen, or camels* (below)

144

still making the things they used to make," he added proudly. "My father's vases are as good as any of the old ones. But the archaeologists say they aren't worth anything. They want to hurt our business. It isn't justice. The stupid tourists pay just as well for the new vases as for the ones that aren't so old."

Megdi considered this matter. He thought of the chipped-away face he had seen in the tomb. But he did not want to talk about that just now. Then he remembered his scarab. "Have you ever been in the young king's tomb?" he asked.

"Which one do you mean?"

"The Pharaoh whose name is on our scarab."

Achmed fished the scarab out of its leather bag.

"Tutankhamen," Megdi read.

"Can you read those signs?" Jacob asked in astonishment.

"Only the names of a few kings," Megdi said.

He drew a second cartouche in the ground and wrote the name "Pepi" inside the ring. "Pepi," he said, "was a Pharaoh who came to the throne at the age of six and lived to be a hundred!" He told them the story of the *dng*. Achmed and Jacob laughed heartily.

"How do you know all that stuff?" Jacob asked.

"From Gurgar," Megdi said. "He has told me even more than my father. But I have learned a great deal from my father, too. There is the story of the man from the salt field, for example." Megdi launched on the tale with so much enthusiasm that Titi let the camel stand and came and sat down where she could hear the

Opposite: *Owner of the tomb hunting in papyrus thicket; tomb of Nakht in Qurna*

story too. Megdi paid no attention. He went on: "And Pharaoh rejoiced in what the man from the salt field had said, more than in anything else he had ever heard. And of course the man was given back his donkeys, and the villain Thutnakht who thought himself so clever was given the beating he deserved, and Pharaoh drove him out into the desert to live or die with the jackals and vultures!"

"Let us hope so!" a deep voice behind Megdi spoke. Megdi whirled around and saw Gurgar. None of them had noticed his approach. "So it should have been," the old man commented. "But unfortunately the end of the story has been lost, and what we have of it says nothing about a beating."

"But my father thinks it must have ended that way," Megdi said.

"I am not so sure," Gurgar replied. "The closer a man is to the sun, the warmer he is: the closer to Pharaoh, the better. The man from the salt field was very far from Pharaoh. How far could his eloquence have helped him? It saved his skin but I doubt that it would have elevated him above a steward of an estate. In the world of ancient Egypt, each man kept to his place. Even artists and craftsmen, despite the fact that their work was highly esteemed, were treated as the lower orders. They had little freedom. They had to live in a special place, a hidden city."

"A hidden city! I've never heard anything about that," Achmed said.

"I could show it to you," Gurgar proposed.

"Fine!" the boys exclaimed all at once. "Can we go right away?"

"Let us make it three o'clock," Gurgar said. "We'll meet in front of Sheik Ali's house. We'd all better have some lunch first, don't you think?"

146

Megdi had no objections. Jacob, Achmed, and Titi, too, suddenly wondered what their mothers would have in the cooking pot. Achmed unhitched the camel. As Gurgar and Megdi walked away together, the old man looked more closely at the boy.

"You were fighting, weren't you?" he said.

"Just a little scrap," Megdi replied evasively.

"What about? Gurgar asked.

"Just a friendly wrestle," Megdi said.

"Little devil!" Gurgar patted Megdi on the back. "You seem to be getting on pretty well with them."

"Pretty well," Megdi said. He did not mention the affair of the scarabs.

He cleaned up as best he could before coming to the table. His father, however, did not fail to notice certain telltale smudges on Megdi's shirt. "You look a bit battered," he said.

"Just a friendly wrestle," Gurgar replied for Megdi. "Otherwise everything is going swimmingly. This afternoon we four will take a look at Der el Medineh."

"You four?"

"Yes," Gurgar said. "Achmed and Jacob want to go along with us to see the hidden city."

THE HIDDEN CITY

Jacob was the first to arrive in the sheik's compound, where they had agreed to meet. Achmed, too, came well before the appointed time, and Gurgar had a cup of coffee brought for each of the boys before they set out. They tramped some distance across the barren height which sloped away to the south, and then turned north.

"There it is," Gurgar said, pointing to the remains of walls, most of them not even the height of a man.

"Is that the hidden city?" Achmed asked, visibly disappointed. Jacob and Megdi, too, looked around for something more extraordinary. They saw only house foundations, arranged in orderly fashion side by side, and courtyard walls of brick made from Nile mud. Many of the walls had crumbled. The settlement, squeezed into a gorge in which there grew not a tree or clump of grass, was bounded on two sides by bare, rocky cliffs.

"It reminds me of a prison," Megdi said.

"Or a cemetery," Achmed added sourly.

"It was a sort of prison," Gurgar said, "and they had a cemetery of their own, as well. We will look at that later." They had entered

148

the eerie ruins and Gurgar led the three boys up a street which had once been lined with houses. The pattern of each house, the number of its rooms, could be made out from the remains of the walls. Some floors were intact, and there were stumps of pillars and walls with traces of paintings.

"You can see that some of the people had finer houses than others," Gurgar commented. "There were differences in wealth: chief sculptors, court cabinet-makers, and so on, lived with a good deal of style. Then there were ordinary workers. The one-room places belonged to them."

Gurgar pointed to a series of walls that lay to one side of the main settlement. "There was a well over there, and next to it a guardhouse, for nothing was more important to this city in the desert than water. Today the well has dried up, but in those days it served the needs of the entire community. They were goldsmiths, carpenters, sandal-makers, painters who lived here—artisans of every sort. Silver and gold, copper and tin were brought in by camels, no doubt, to be heated, alloyed, smelted, laid on the anvil and beaten out, cut into rings. Blocks of malachite, cornelian and lapis lazuli were brought in, to be cut and polished. Statues were hewn out of granite and limestone blocks, vessels shaped out of alabaster. It seems a quiet place now, but it must have been very different. The air must have resounded with the myriad noises of the workshops. There were furnaces and open fires beside which men crouched with bellows, fanning the fires to greater heat; bronze doors, statues, and statuettes were being poured. In the workshops of the carpenters bronze saws would be eating into the trunks of trees, cutting out boards and beams. Skilled joiners would

149

inlay coloured woods into handsome chests and cabinets, armchairs, tables, bedsteads. They polished their wood with sandstone, they carved, they glued. They even made plywood of as many as six layers! Glassworkers poured molten glass and blew fine glass vessels. Potters turned jars on their wheels. Shoemakers produced precious sandals with the faces of Asiatics, Negroes, and Libyans on the soles. Weavers turned out soft warm blankets and the finest fabrics upon their looms. The men in these workshops understood their crafts. Sons learned from fathers; this city was a school which went on for centuries."

"It must have been a pretty lively place," Achmed said, with a touch of envy.

"The whole region was lively," Gurgar said. "The rock cliffs were quarries which echoed with the clamour of hammers and saws and drills; the city streets smelled of molten metal, burned oil, and sweat. But the city must have gloried in its noise and toil, for all that was beautiful and precious in the Two Kingdoms stemmed from here. The artists and craftsmen who lived crowded together in this place were capable of mastering every task that Pharaoh or the powerful nobles of the kingdom set them to. They sailed to Aswân and Hammamat and opened up the mountains, broke from them blocks of stone weighing tons, even whole obelisks."

"How could they do it?" Megdi asked. "They didn't have dynamite in those days, did they?"

"No," Gurgar said. "But they drove special wedges of very dry wood into carefully chiselled holes, and then poured water over the wedges. After ten hours or so the rock wall would groan and split, and an obelisk would lie free. Those ancient quarrymen overcame the resistance of even the toughest granite with the power of swelling wood. And when they had hewn their colossal stones, they managed to move them. They brought the massive figures down the Nile on rafts and boats, dragged them long distances on sleds, or what are called stone-boats, dragged by 50, 100, or even 150 men. Feats which today strike us as impossible were the order of the day for them."

"Were these the same people who did the actual building of the pyramids?" Megdi asked.

"They must have come from this same city. When summoned by their masters, they went forth and took charge of the building of those 'gateways into the netherworld.' Secret mountain paths, of which the ordinary people knew nothing, led from this craftsmen's city to the valleys of the kings and queens, and to the cliffs in which the nobles had their tombs. In the scheme of things in ancient Egypt, the artists and craftsmen were indispensable. Who else could insure men life after death? They had a special name for the artist; he was called 'he who creates life.' Rightly so, for the Pharaohs, queens, nobles, musicians, and servants whom they carved in stone or cast in bronze or portrayed in paint are as alive today as they were thousands of years ago."

"Not always," Megdi put in with great presence of mind. "In certain tombs the paintings have faded, or been defaced."

Gurgar looked meaningfully at each of the boys. "That is true," he said. "What a blow it would have been to the owners of the tombs, had they been able to imagine that all their efforts to fix forever their images on the walls of their tombs were to be wasted. How much care they devoted to the thing! A painting or a statue

151

had to be accurate down to the last finger. If a donkey with a load were shown, the lid of the pannier would be painted open so that the owner of the donkey could make sure at a glance that nothing was missing. The owner of the tomb commanded: Let there be a table set with all manner of food. The painter painted, and the table was set—for all time to come. Or the landowner ordered: Show my favourite hunting and fishing spots, and the sculptor took chisel in his hand and carved a relief of reeds and water, ducks and a school of fish, out of the naked rock. There it was, whatever the master would need for his eternal recreation. Nothing was lacking, for all times to come.

"The Pharaohs, queens, and dignitaries appreciated such work. They were not stingy in proofs of their favour. The artists received gold and praise, precious chains and titles. In a master-builder's tomb a golden ell has been found: a measuring stick made of massive gold. It was a gift from Amenophis II to the man who built for him. But the greatest privilege of all was the permission given to these masters to erect an eternal house for themselves and their families, a tomb no less splendid than those of viziers and other highly placed officials. The builders and architects, too, were mighty men, men who 'preserved life.' Come, let us look."

Gurgar led the boys over to the western slope opposite the towering pyramid which had not been built by human hands. There were tombs on this western slope, and in front of them, like guards, stood little pyramids, dwarfs compared to the tombs of the Pharaohs, but still signs of great dignity.

They entered the eternal house of Chief Sculptor Senudyem. It

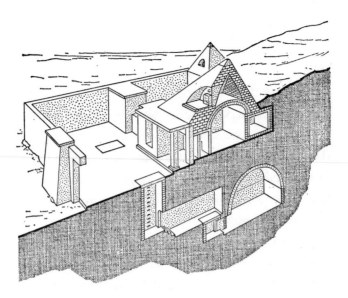

Tomb with dwarf pyramid in Der el Medineh (section)

was one of the lucky exceptions which had never been looted.
When it was found, it was filled with a variety of household utensils
which showed that Senudyem was no ordinary man. On the walls
his transfer to the West was portrayed, and his life in those realms
where the grain grew sixteen ells high and there was never lack of
water. His wife was at his side, sharing all the joys with him. In the
tomb of one of Senudyem's two sons, Gurgar pointed to a painting:

"See, that is Anubis, the god of the dead. He is bending over
Osiris to assure him that he will arise again to a new life. The
mummy of Osiris, which usually has a human form, is pictured
than a fish?"

"Why?" the boys asked.

153

"The ancients regarded the Nile as the bringer of life," the ol[d] man explained. "Therefore who could be more surrounded by lif[e] than a fish?"

They went on from picture to picture, and Gurgar always wa[s] able to explain what ideas were concealed within the painting[s]. Now and then he would glance at Achmed and Jacob to see ho[w] they were responding. They were neither bored nor scornful now[;] in fact, they were as eager as Megdi to know all that Gurgar coul[d] tell them. When their tour of the hidden city was over, they wer[e] plainly disappointed.

"Aren't we very near the Valley of the Queens now?" Megd[i] asked. "Couldn't we go and look at it?"

"That is not something which can be done in the tail end of a[n] afternoon," Gurgar said. "Some of the tombs are more splendi[d] than many a Pharaoh's grave. Especially the chambers of Quee[n] Nefertiti, the wife of Ikhnaton."

They left the hidden city by crossing the ridges that bounded i[t] on the east. From the top the view opened out over plain an[d] Nile as far as Luxor and Karnak. Above the rich green of th[e] fields the remains of the temples rose resplendently, glowing as if th[e] walls were plated with gold.

"There once was a great deal of real gold on those walls," Gurgar said. "But it has long since been taken away, like every[-] thing else that could be turned into money. I wish we could hav[e] only a single glimpse of the temples of Ramses the Great and hi[s] son when they were still intact—places of unimaginable magnifi[-] cence."

Achmed looked back at the hidden city below them. "Remem[-]

er what you said before?" he asked suddenly. "That the city was artly a prison?"

"That was so," Gurgar replied. "The artisans of the city were ighly thought of. They were often honoured, but also guarded. hey were locked within this city for their whole lives, except when iey went out on special missions."

"But couldn't they have run away?"

"Probably they did not mind their imprisonment," Gurgar anwered.

"How can you tell?"

"I think we can tell from their works," Gurgar said. "There is othing in the works which shows anything but a joy in their own reative talents."

"Isn't there anything written about those artisans?" Megdi asked. Like the story of the man from the salt field?"

"Oh yes," Gurgar said. "The ancient Egyptians wrote about verything imaginable. They considered writing more important han ploughing or weaving, painting or building temples. At any ate the scribes thought so. They had developed the art of writing, nd they lived to use it. It is amazing enough how much has been ritten, and incredible how much has come to light again."

Gurgar pointed to the low ground between the hidden city and ie tombs of the dignitaries. "Over in that area an excavator found deep well which was filled to the top with broken pieces of brick nd stone. A whole well full of shards. And there were marks of riting on many of the pieces. The excavator and his helpers set bout putting the pieces together. In the end that is what it always omes to." He stopped and gripped Achmed's arm. "Imagine yourself finding a few pages of a book; you start to read, are caught up in the story, and yet you have only two or three pages; all the rest has been torn out of the book and scattered by the wind. But here and there you see a page lying around. What do you do?"

"Gather them up," Achmed said. "Until . . ."

"Until you have the rest of the book, and then you read it,' Gurgar finished for him. "You see, that is just what the archaeologists do. They come upon bits and pieces, carefully dig them out and put together the things that belong together, bit by bit, until in the end they have whole stories like the story of the *dng* or the man from the salt field, or even the practice exercises scribes had to write when they were going to school and learning to be scribes. The idea was pounded into the heads of ancient schoolboys that no calling on earth was greater than that of a scribe.

"Once upon a time, a man named Duauf brought his son Pepi to the school for scribes. For parting words, he told the boy to love his books more than he loved his own mother. The little lecture that this Duauf gave his sons was dear to the heart of all future school-teachers. So much so that they must have assigned it to all their pupils, generation after generation. The same text crops up time and again on shards dating from a number of different centuries. 'Believe me, my son,' so went the piece, 'all palaces belong to the scribe. Never have I seen a sculptor or goldsmith who was sent to kings. The scribe stands high above all others, no matter what their occupation. For consider this: The founder stands ever at the gate to an inferno. His hands are rough as the skin of a crocodile; he smells worse than a fish. Every evening the stonemason drops with exhaustion, and merchants are bitten by the mosquitoes in the delta
156

he bricklayer spends all day handling the Nile mud, and he lives with the cattle. The gardener works himself to death; in the morning he waters the leeks and in the evening the vines. And the farmer? In all eternity he is never out of debt; he is as well off as a deer among lions. Mice and locusts and sparrows cheat him of the fruits of his toil. The worm eats half of what remains, and the hippopotamus the rest. When the scribe lands in his boat to collect the taxes accompanied by Negro helpers wielding clubs, he gives the order: "Deliver the grain!" And the farmer replies: "There is none left!" Whereupon he is stretched on the ground and beaten. Therefore be a scribe! And certainly not a fisherman! The crocodiles lie in wait for him. Nor a chariot soldier, nor an army officer! For the soldier is sent off to the barracks while still a child. On the march through the mountains he is laden like a donkey and drinks stinking water. Exhausted, he confronts the enemy. A burning blow strikes him; a wound springs open on his head. His body is dead even while he still lives. If he ever comes home to Egypt, he is like wood already eaten by worms. Therefore be a scribe! All others have someone above themselves—a scribe. Only the scribe has no one over him; he stands above all others, supervises their work. Therefore learn, write with your hand and read with your mouth. Put your heart into your books and be diligent, for otherwise you will learn that a boy's ear is on his back.' "

"A boy's ear is on his back?" Jacob puzzled over this.

Gurgar was all prepared to illustrate what he meant. "I see, I see," Jacob cried just in time.

"What the schoolboy exercise said was true," Gurgar went on. "The scribe was really in a unique position in Egypt. The highest

157

offices were open to him. A scribe could become a grand vizier. Whatever hardships might overtake the other classes of the population, a scribe never had to go hungry. Even the artisans in the hidden city—who were a privileged group on every count even if they were virtually prisoners—sometimes suffered from the periodic famines which would sweep the country."

"What would they do about it?" Achmed asked with keen interest. "Would they just stay in their city and starve to death?"

"We know of one such occasion," Gurgar said. "It took place in the twenty-ninth year of the reign of the third Ramses. The entire month of Tybi had passed without new rations being brought to the people in the hidden city. All their food had been consumed. They waited patiently for nine days more. Then they broke out of their city, which was surrounded by five walls. The full population of men, women, and children marched against a temple. They knew that food supplies were kept in its storerooms. There they sat down and refused to go away.

"The scribes and priests came out of the temple and attempted to pacify them with 'great oaths.' Still the people refused to abandon their siege of the temple. The following day, moreover, they advanced upon a still bigger temple, the Ramesseum. 'We have come because of hunger and thirst,' they said. 'We have neither bread nor fish, let alone sufficient clothes for our bodies. We demand that the vizier and Pharaoh be told of this.' Seeing their resolution, the priests finally distributed food. That was on the thirteenth day of Mekhir. The people returned to the city, trusting the promises of the officials. But in the following month of Phamenoth things were as bad as ever and they were once more forgotten.

Again they broke out of their city and informed the temple priests and officials: 'We have crossed the walls not only because of our hunger. We have come to speak a terrible truth: In this place which is Pharaoh's, injustice has been done.' The vizier came forth. He attempted to quiet the demonstrators with a few sacks of grain. The people then prepared to storm the port. The scribe Amennakht threatened to cast every rebel into prison. Finally a compromise was reached, and after having received the rations that were due to them, the people returned to the city."

"And all this is written down somewhere?" asked Achmed.

"It is written down," Gurgar said. "And it is not the only account of this sort that has been found."

"That's because they had scribes," Jacob said. "Otherwise no one would know of such happenings."

The sun vanished behind El Qurn. The air turned swiftly cool. They had been walking back toward Qurna and were now approaching Sheik Ali's house.

"What about tomorrow?" Achmed asked at the gate. "Will you take us somewhere tomorrow?"

"Don't you have to run the water wheel?" Gurgar inquired.

"Oh, that's Titi's job," Achmed replied, without a moment's scruple. "We just turn everything over to Titi. She's a pretty smart girl." He winked at Jacob.

"What else is she so smart about?" Megdi wanted to know.

"You can always trust Titi to make the best deal," Achmed said. "My father and mother couldn't do without her. She's wonderful at selling to the tourists. She'll sit out along the road with a couple of vases made by my father. Of course we have a little sign

159

reading 'Imitations'—that's the law. But Titi looks so picturesque
that the tourists always stop. And the funny thing is that as soon
as the tourists come, that sign disappears. The tourists are always
glad to buy from her. They don't buy half as much from me or my
father."

"Scoundrelly tricks," Gurgar growled. But the laughter-wrinkles
at the corners of his eyes deepened. "Well then, let us meet in Dai al
Bahri tomorrow morning—half past six at the latest. At that hour
I think no one will be there—aside from the queen whom we intend to visit."

INCENSE AND WEAPONS

Neither Achmed nor Jacob had ever before been in Dai al-Bahri at that hour of the morning. It was beautifully quiet. The temple clung to the vertical wall of the cliff. They were looking down upon it from above, for Gurgar had led them along the steep path which connects the gorge of Dai al-Bahri with the Valley of the Kings. From this height they could view a whole row of ruined temples on the borderline between the fields and the desert. Beyond lay the wide Theban valley, the Nile, Luxor, and Karnak.

"All that once belonged together," Gurgar said. "In the days of her splendour, Thebes was actually a twin city. Over there was the city of the living, and here in the desert the city of the dead. The two were connected by avenues of sphinxes which ran from temple to temple. Mighty ramps led from the edges of the valley to the eternal dwellings in the rocky cliffs, and there were festival highways lined with alabaster chapels for the barges in which the gods pay visits to one another. Gods and men crossed the Nile in holy barges to celebrate 'the beautiful feast in the desert valley.' Thebes was called the City of the Hundred Gates. Everyone in the New

161

Kingdom knew that she was the centre of the world. Similarly, the complex of temples at Karnak was known to be the greatest of all sacred places. It was called 'the counter of places,' because all other sanctuaries were subject to it. Pharaoh after Pharaoh added to the temple, each one striving to surpass his predecessors with the height of his temple gates and the length of his temple halls. These were the same kings who extended Egypt's borders far into Asia and Africa. They conceived of themselves as generals for a god who had dictated that all other lands be subject to Egypt. Within their temples they erected monuments to the victories they had won for this god, who had many names—Amen, Ra, Min—and many forms. Karnak, Luxor, the Ramesseum, Medinet Habu—these temples were all fortresses of the gods, built by militant kings who had subjected half the known world to their sway. The peoples of two continents trembled before them. And no wonder, for at a word of command, forests of great pillars sprang up for them, colonnades fit for giants. Their obelisks pierced the firmament like monstrous lances with golden tips, landmarks for the Sun. The buildings erected by Ramses the Great and his son on the western shore were both temples and palaces in one, titanic castles in which stood stone colossi weighing a thousand tons and more, cut out of the wonderful red stone to the north of Heliopolis and transported upstream 450 miles.

"Thus, all the temples of Thebes were arrogant structures, boastful, blatant assertions of power. This one is the single exception." Gurgar looked down at the temple of Dai al-Bahri. "About this one there is nothing boastful. It fits in so perfectly here that it seems to have been born out of the mountain. See the way its broad ter
162

races spread open to the sky. The façades were pierced by door upon door, and all stood open so that the light was freely admitted to the temple. Gently rising ramps invited the worshipper to ascend. In the midst of this rocky wasteland a garden was conjured up filled with flowering trees brought from distant places, wherein the god could refresh himself. For it was a queen who built this temple, and it was evidently her intention to create here a little bit of the paradise which the ancient Egyptians called Punt, the land of incense. She was a ruler in her own right and her name was Hatshepsut, which means 'Highest of all noble women.' And if ever a queen deserved such a name, she did."

Gurgar sat down on a flat stone and the three boys settled down around his feet. The sun had risen far enough above the horizon so that it was beginning to cast some warmth. In the early light the tremendous cliff against which the temple nestled came alive with tender shades of rose and ochre.

"Ancient Egypt," Gurgar recounted, "had no lack of great queens. The name of Cleopatra is still known to us, centuries after her death. We have a lasting image of that beautiful young queen with whom the two great Romans, Caesar and Mark Antony, fell in love. No matter how little we know about ancient Egypt, we know it had a queen named Cleopatra. Significantly enough, it was her name, chiselled into the Rosetta stone, which provided Champollion with a key for deciphering hieroglyphics.

"Cleopatra came at the very end of Egypt's greatness. At the end of almost all the dynasties the reins of government passed to the hands of women. They bridged the gap between one dynasty and the next. Even in times of defeat they preserved their dignity.

163

The Greeks wrote with great admiration of the resolute Queen Nitokris, who sat on the throne of the Pharaohs when the Old Kingdom finally collapsed. The Pharaoh was killed by a group of conspirators. The kingdom was plunged into chaos, with seventy kings installed and unseated in as many days. How long were the rival groups to go on warring with each other? Nitokris saw but one choice. She invited the conspirators to a feast from which none departed alive, including herself.

"Five hundred years later the two lands were again rocked to their foundations. Internal dissension had so weakened Egypt that foreign tribes from Asia seized the chance to invade. Mounted hordes who called themselves Hyksos established a stronghold at the north-eastern corner of the delta, and from that base succeeded in subjugating all Egypt. Or almost all, for in time certain strong figures at the southern gate of Egypt rose in rebellion. There were two kings named Tao who attempted to throw off the yoke of oppression. Wars were fought against the foreign usurpers. The second Tao, who was called 'He who was made brave by Ra,' fell in battle—his mummy is marked by fatal wounds. Yet still his line persisted in the struggle. One of his sons rallied around himself the princes he could count on. He addressed them: 'I should like to know what I am good for if I permit an Asiatic to sit in Auaris, in Cush a Nubian. I shall save Egypt and defeat the Asiatics and the Negroes!'

"Once more, he pitted his forces against the Hyksos. He did not live to see their expulsion, but his brother drove the foreigners out of the delta. His brother's successor, Amenophis, completed the liberation, and became founder of the Eighteenth Dynasty. Revi-
164

talized by the long struggle against their foreign rulers, the Pharaoh's people now burst forth out of their borders. War followed war. Thutmose I penetrated the lands to the south, marching through valleys where no previous Pharaoh had ever set foot. At the end of his reign, Egypt extended from the 'Horn of the Earth,' the Fourth Cataract, as far as the frontiers of Asia. With horses and war chariots which the Egyptians had taken over from their oppressors, Egyptian armies invaded foreign lands and themselves became oppressors. Bands of prisoners without number were driven like herds of sheep into the Land of the Nile; like cattle they were branded with burning irons to mark their ownership. In addition to the army of charioteers and infantry, increased by mercenaries from Libya and Cush and the Asiatic provinces, there was henceforth an army of slaves in the land of the Pharaohs.

"Such was the world into which Hatshepsut was born. She was the only child of the warlike Thutmose and his queen Ahmose, who was his half-sister. Many Pharaohs were the children of such brother-and-sister marriages, in imitation of Horus, whose father Osiris and mother Isis were brother and sister. The real father of every Pharaoh was considered to be the god who ruled over heaven and earth. In the hall of birth of the temple of Dai al-Bahri, we may read: 'The god came who is lord over all, even over the throne of the two lands, and he approached the queen in the shape of her husband, King Thutmose. Amid the splendours of the palace, he found her sleeping. Awakened by the perfume which enveloped the king, she was glad, and he went up to her and burned for love of her. And when he had come closer to her, she saw how he was like a god, and she rejoiced.'

"When the hour of birth neared, the goddess Hathor led the queen before Amen so that his child would see the light of the world in his godly presence.

"This child was Hatshepsut. She remained the only child of the bride of the god. Thutmose also had a son, but he was born to one of the lesser wives. Though he ascended the throne as Thutmose II he actually became Pharaoh through the marriage to his half-sister. For *she* had been presented to Amen as the future Pharaoh, and the statue of the god had accepted her as such by graciously nodding its head. Whereupon the nobles and the people kissed the ground upon which the princess had stood.

"When Thutmose II died, he left behind a young son who had been born to him by a woman of his harem. This son was ultimately to become Thutmose III. For the present, however, he was given no royal dignities at all, and had to serve in a temple in Thebes. The queen Hatshepsut assumed all the powers of government, and reigned as Pharaoh. In a history of this period which a dignitary of the kingdom had chiselled into the walls of his tomb, we may read:

" 'Queen Hatshepsut cared for the land and governed it according to her will. All Egypt submitted to her rule, for she had sprung from the god himself, and her administration was excellent. She considered it her task to heal the wounds which the two lands had suffered during the time of foreign rulers. So she restored the things that had been destroyed when the Asiatics ruled in the city of Auaris. They ruled who did not recognize Ra and the order of Heaven.'

"Hatshepsut was a great queen but with her gentle, womanly nature she could not bring herself to send forth her armies to de-
166

vastate other countries. She did not dispatch her fleets to ravage their coasts, but to exchange peacefully the goods of one country for the goods of the others. In the ninth year of her reign she sent ships to the incense land of Punt. There are indications that during her time a canal running along the Wadi Tumilat connected the Nile directly with the Red Sea. Perhaps it had been constructed with just such commerce in mind.

"This voyage to Punt is charmingly depicted in a series of paintings and texts in the Punt Hall of the temple. To honour the god, the queen had decided to prepare a land of Punt on the soil of Thebes. Indeed, he had commanded her to do so, and to make it large enough so that he could stroll in it. 'Seek out ways to Punt and open the paths to the mountains of myrrh!' the god's voice had said to her in the sanctuary of the temple.

"Hatshepsut set about at once equipping the expedition. Five barges, each with a set of sails and thirty oarsmen, were laden with provisions and gifts, bales of cloth, and jars of beverages. A sacrifice was made to Hathor, the goddess of Punt. Then the queen's fleet set sail toward the east. The winds were favourable.

"When the expedition at last arrived on the coast of Punt, the Egyptians were struck with amazement. Among incense trees stood huts shaped like beehives, set upon high piles so that the inhabitants would be safe from wild beasts and enemy attacks. Ladders led up to the openings, which served as doors. On the ground beneath these strange habitations grazed donkeys, and cattle with blunt horns. But strangest of all were the inhabitants of Punt, people with brown faces, free-flowing hair, and clipped beards. Great was their amazement when the Egyptians left their ships. 'How have you come here,' they asked, 'to a land that no one knows of? Have you fallen from the sky?'

"Paruhu, the reigning prince of Punt, came forward to meet the visitors, followed by his wife mounted on a donkey. The princess was so fat that she was not permitted to take a step. She had to be helped off the donkey. With difficulty she stood on her legs long enough to greet the guests.

"The trading proceeded swiftly. The Egyptians set up tables by the seashore and heaped daggers, axes, and necklaces upon them. A statue of Queen Hatshepsut together with the god Amen was given to the prince as a gift. In the envoys' tent a feast was served of all the good food produced by the Land of the Nile. Then boards were laid from shore to ships to form gangplanks, and the sailors hastily loaded their ships with all that the people of Punt had brought as gifts: heaps of incense, ebony and ivory, the white gold from the land of Amu, fragrant woods, hides, eye paint, baboons, long-tailed monkeys, greyhounds, slaves, and children. The ships were loaded high with the treasures of the land of Punt, and with all the most beautiful plants from this land. Never before had the like been brought to any queen, we are assured. On the homeward voyage the monkeys were set free. They cavorted about the ship and clambered up the masts, to the immense delight of the sailors.

"There was great rejoicing when the ships at last docked in Thebes. Thirty-one incense trees had survived the long voyage, and these now took root on the terraces of the temple. There ponds bordered by papyrus reeds had been laid out, and at the gate stood persea trees as green guardians. The like of this garden was

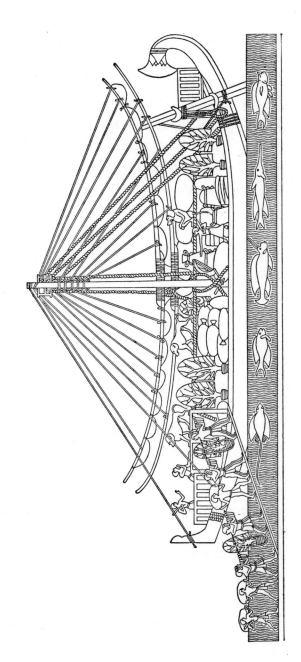

Loading of a ship before the departure from Punt (from the temple of Hatshepsut in Dai al-Bahri)

not to be seen in the two Thebes. Hatshepsut had created a dupli-cate of Punt in the desert!

"Hatshepsut not only had Dai al-Bahri built, she also provided for other temples, in particular the temple of Karnak. Indeed, as she herself declared, she could not sleep because of this temple, so dear to her heart was it. In the centre of it she had two obelisks erected; one of them, a hundred feet tall and hewn out of a single block of red granite, stands to this day. The peaks of these obelisks were covered with pure gold and 'mingled with the sky' when the sun cast its first glance upon them in the morning.

"We happen to know who transported these obelisks from the quarry at Aswân, for he left a statue of himself in the temple. This same man succeeded in placing the obelisks in the midst of the many pillars of Karnak, and he too built the temple of Dai al-Bahri—the first of its kind; in this he resembled Imhotep who built the first pyramid. Hatshepsut's architect was named Sennemut. He was a brother of the queen's tutor. She early recognized his great gifts and placed her building projects in his charge. Ultimately this architect became her closest adviser. She entrusted to him the edu-cation of her only daughter, who was perhaps also his daughter. For Sennemut stood closer to the queen than her half-brother, who was her husband in name; and after her brother's early death Sennemut was the uncrowned Pharaoh, enjoying the love and the unqualified confidence of the queen. What lesser man would have dared to place his statue in her mortuary temple whose walls had room otherwise only for gods and kings? And how else would he have dared have the statue show him with his arms around little Prin-cess Nefrure, and her little head resting against his? He is also men-

170

ioned in connection with the voyage to Punt, and possibly he was he one who first suggested this dramatic venture.

"During the excavations of 1927-28 under the direction of the American archaeologist Winlock an exciting discovery was made at Dai al-Bahri. A shaft was found which began a long distance in front of the terraces of the temple and went down to a great depth. This shaft was traced to its end and led to a vault which lay directly under the spot where the funeral sacrifice for Hatshepsut would be placed. This was the secret tomb of Sennemut. He had had another tomb erected for himself in the area reserved for dignitaries of the court, but that other tomb was only a sham. His real sarcophagus stood ready in this secret chamber beneath the temple. Sennemut wanted—and surely it was Hatshepsut's wish—to be buried in the mortuary temple of his queen and his beloved.

"Further excavations showed that this desire was never fulfilled. The sarcophagus was found smashed. Sennemut was never interred within it. Neither was he honourably interred in his other tomb. Sennemut and all his kinsfolk, all his servants and his pets, in fact everything that could possibly be a reminder of his existence, were wiped from the face of the earth. That was done in the year 1469 B.C."

"But who did it, and why?" Achmed asked breathlessly.

"The man who had been forced into the background for more than twenty years. Now his chance came to strike and take revenge. I am speaking of Thutmose III, who had waited all these years in the shadows. Mediocre himself, passed over, ignored, how he must have hated his brilliant rival. How, equally, he must have hated the woman who was his stepmother, his aunt, and nominally his wife. Born to rule, he burned with the lust for power. Amen himself, he believed, had called him to throne by an oracle. But he bided his time until he could be sure of every detail of his plot. For the queen was loved, and all her followers were loyal. At last he was ready to strike. What form his uprising took, we do not know, but we know that it was extraordinarily ferocious. He was not content with slaughtering the queen and her unofficial consort; he raged like a madman against everything that remained of her. Wherever he found a painting of the woman he hated, he had it cut out of the wall. He destroyed her statues, whether they showed her as Pharaoh or in the form of a sphinx, by having them heated with fire and then abruptly cooled with water, so that they burst. The archaeologist Winlock found the ruins of these statues in a quarry. Out of fragments of pink granite and limestone he reconstructed the figure of the great queen—thus conferring a new life upon her after three and a half millennia.

"Her sarcophagus, too, was found empty, just like Sennemut's. Perhaps Thutmose III killed the queen with his own hand and in the frenzy of his hatred had her corpse thrown to the dogs; that was commonly done with outlaws, in order to deprive them of all possibility of a life in the afterworld. Hundreds of desecrations of the walls of temples show the thoroughness of Thutmose's revenge.

"Like Sennemut, the queen had had two tombs prepared for herself. One of these was discovered by Carter in 1916. From the foot of a hidden crack in a cliff a passage was driven twenty yards deep through solid rock until it met a shaft. At the bottom of this shaft was found an unfinished sarcophagus made of crystalline sandstone. This was evidently an early tomb, abandoned after Hatshep-

172

ut became Pharaoh in her own right.
Carter also found the other, grander
omb, located in the Valley of the Kings.
Here, too, the sarcophagus was empty.
By measurements he determined that the
even-hundred-foot passage to the sar-
ophagus chamber was lined up precisely
with a prolongation of the ramp to the
emple of Dai al-Bahri. This meant that a
ecret passageway had been cut through
he mountain ridge over which El Qurn
owers. Through this passage the queen
would have been able to go from her sar-
ophagus chamber to her temple. But her
enemy had destroyed this passage, also.
Not a trace of her was to remain; not a
single wish of hers was to be fulfilled. The
desecration was to be complete. But in
his Thutmose failed. Enough remained
of the Punt garden which Hatshepsut and
Sennemut had planted in the desert of
Thebes to keep alive the name of the gra-
cious-spirited queen. And of her two obelisks, one still stands. They were too

*Horus name of Queen Hatshepsut; underneath
—inserted later—the name of Thutmose III*

mighty and sacred to be levelled. All Thutmose dared do was to enclose them in a wall, as if to hide them from sight. Yet to this day the tip of the obelisk gleams as though covered with gold as soon as the sun rises above the horizon.

"There is one inscription in the temple of Karnak set there by Hatshepsut. 'I am the raging crocodile whose jaws snap, and there is no escape for him whom they seize.' It is not an appropriate inscription. Perhaps she had it put there when she began to feel herself threatened. But in fact violence was alien to her nature. Thutmose was the raging crocodile. Once he had secured the throne for himself, the shadowy mediocrity proved a savage ruler. Of the thirty-two years during which he ruled alone, twenty were occupied by military campaigns. He extended the southern border of Egypt far southward and created a new province between the second and the fourth cataracts of the Nile. This was called Cush, and was ruled by a governor who was known as the 'King's Son of Cush,' appointed by the Pharaoh. The conquered lands of Nubia and Cush supplied him with money and soldiers for fresh conquests. On the walls of the temple of Karnak he boasted of seventeen campaigns and claimed that he led his army as far as the 'rivers which flow backwards,' the Tigris and the Euphrates."

"Why 'rivers which flow backwards'?" Jacob asked. "What does that mean?"

"The Tigris and the Euphrates," Gurgar explained, "flow from north to south. But to an ancient Egyptian the only proper way for a river to flow was from south to north, like the Nile. But to go on about Thutmose: his pent-up ambition had something terrible about it. Moreover, he was a born leader of armies. War was his
174

element. When he marched upon Megiddo, his generals advised him against attacking by way of the narrow pass at Carmel because in such a spot a handful of defenders could shatter his forces. What do you think this king did? He gave his men the choice of following him or turning back, and he himself pressed on the route 'on which no one will expect us because it is too dangerous.' As he had reasoned, the enemy was thrown into total confusion. From this one battle, he returned with great booty: the account of the campaign lists 2,041 horses, numberless chariots, great treasures, a year's harvest. The defeated princes, who had come to battle in splendid chariots, rode back home on donkeys. Thutmose took their sons as hostages into Egypt to be reared and educated in all respects like Egyptians, and when, one by one, the Asiatic princes died, the Pharaoh installed these willing pawns on the vacant thrones.

"In the course of all these military campaigns, the king accumulated unprecedented wealth in slaves, cattle, and treasures. Gold was heaped up in the treasuries of the palaces and temples. In addition to the gold which came into the country as tribute, slaves toiled in the mines to extract new gold. Perhaps in emulation of the queen whom he had murdered, Thutmose III was a passionate collector. He had his artists represent on the walls of temples the many strange animals, plants, and flowers which he had brought to Egypt from distant places. He extended the horizon of the Egyptians far out over the deserts in the east and west, over the sea in the north and beyond the cataracts in the south. Thutmose transformed Egypt into a mighty empire which held sway over lands far beyond its borders. One of his viziers attested: 'Everything

which happened. the king knew. There was nothing he wished
that he could not find a way to accomplish, nothing he undertook
that he did not carry to a conclusion. On earth he was Thoth, the
all-knowing.'

"It was the fashion, under Thutmose, for officers to boast of their
deeds. Their exploits, too, cast honour on the Pharaoh. Hence we
know how a certain Dhuti, a general of Thutmose's, outwitted
the prince of Joppa during the siege of that city. He sent a message
secretly to the prince, promising to desert to him. Moreover he
made ready five hundred panniers laden with gifts which he would
give to the city. Delighted, the prince came out to Dhuti's tent to
celebrate their new friendship. When he was full of wine, the
Egyptian levelled him to the ground with a blow of the king's
club. Then he had donkeys carry the five hundred baskets into the
city. These were the gifts that everyone within the city was expecting and the donkeys entered freely. Armed warriors stepped out
of the baskets—and Joppa fell.

"Another officer of Thutmose, Horemheb by name, boasted that
he had saved his king's life by cutting off the trunk of an elephant
that had attacked Pharaoh. For this deed, he was awarded a gold
badge of honor. . . . Of course, whenever Thutmose himself is
present, he is the bravest of all. We have one chronicle which tells
of his attacking a herd of 120 elephants in the territory of Nii, and if
we are to believe the story, these elephants were doomed as surely
as all the enemies of Pharaoh."

"But if it was written down, don't you believe it?" Achmed pressed.

Opposite: *Hatshepsut, from one of her obelisks in Karnak*

"I know how easy it is to write boastful words and big numbers," Gurgar replied. "Possibly there were only twenty elephants. But if there had been 120, I don't doubt that Thutmose would have attacked them."

"Then you think he was brave," Achmed said.

"He was brave," Gurgar admitted. "He had an almost inhuman courage. As for me, I would sooner have sent ships to the wonderful land of Punt than taken part in that slaughter of elephants."

Gurgar rose from his stone seat. He pointed down into the gorge. "Down there," he said, "was once the beautiful garden of Hatshepsut. In planting it, the queen made the desert bloom. Thutmose, on the other hand, left many a desert behind him when he returned home from his wars." He glanced at the sun to estimate the time. "You boys had better go into the temple now. You won't need me. The walls of the temple will tell you all you want to know."

"But we want you to explain things to us," the boys objected.

"I have an appointment over there," Gurgar said, pointing up the path which led into the Valley of the Kings. Then he left them.

"I know where he's going," Achmed said as the old man passed out of sight. "To the tomb of the Golden Pharaoh."

"Tutankhamen?" Megdi asked in surprise.

Achmed nodded. "The Pharaoh he discovered."

"But wasn't it Carter who discovered the tomb?" Megdi asked.

"The Englishman was all for abandoning the site," Achmed asserted. "It was Gurgar, his reis, who insisted on probing a while longer. Suddenly his shovel struck the first of the sixteen steps."

Opposite: *Nefertiti; unfinished model from Amarna*

177

"He's never said a word to me about that," exclaimed Megdi.

"That is the way Gurgar is," Achmed said. "He never wants anything for himself. Just plain foolish, if you ask me."

They ran down the rocky path.

"It must have looked nice when there was a garden here," Megdi said as they approached the terrace. "And a bit of shade would be welcome right now." They stood before the brilliant scenes depicted on the walls and pointed out to each other various details which Gurgar had prepared them for. Again and again there were blanks in the pictures where the portrait of the queen had been defaced.

"He was a cruel king," Jacob commented. "I don't like him at all. I like the queen much better."

"But he made Egypt greater!" Achmed countered.

This led to a bit of a quarrel. Each of the boys had reacted differently to the stories Gurgar had told about Thutmose III. Jacob was repelled by the savage nature of the great conqueror. Achmed, on the other hand, admired Thutmose III. He kept insisting that a king was great for those very qualities. As Megdi listened to the two of them, he became less and less sure which side he was on. He would ask Father, he finally decided.

His chance came sooner than he expected. The boys were climbing the height which separates Dai al-Bahri from Qurna when they saw a man some little distance below waving to them. It was Megdi's father. He had been working in this terrain all morning inspecting one of the tombs. Achmed and Jacob suddenly became very shy, but Megdi took their hands and made them come along with him. They scrambled down the slope and went running up to the archaeologist.

178

"This is Achmed," Megdi said, "and this is Jacob. We've just been inside the temple of Dai al-Bahri."

"And what did you think of it?" Father asked.

"Achmed is for Thutmose and Jacob is for Hatshepsut," Megdi said. "Who are you for, Father?"

"I am for both," the archaeologist answered. "Both of them did a great deal for Egypt."

Achmed pushed his advantage. "Egypt was surrounded by enemies," he said, "Under the queen she would have become weaker and weaker."

"Not necessarily," Father said. "It's true that the queen sent out no military expeditions. On the other hand, she made a great effort to win the friendship of neighbouring peoples."

"She was just a woman!" Achmed said contemptuously.

"She was not the only monarch of Egypt who deliberately refrained from making war. There was another Pharaoh who did the same thing."

"He couldn't have been much of a Pharaoh," Achmed answered sceptically.

"Many people regard him as the greatest Pharaoh who ever lived," the archaeologist answered.

"Were you planning to work this afternoon?" Megdi inquired with what he thought was subtle duplicity.

Father considered. "You mean you'd like to go to Karnak?" he asked. Megdi nodded boldly. "All right, then," Father said, "I'll show you Karnak. Meet me at the boat two hours from now."

THE HORIZON OF ATEN

Three hours later Achmed and Jacob boarded the excavators' boat, thus breaking all the unwritten laws of the village of Qurna, which dictated that no proper Qurnese should accept a seat in the archaeologists' vessel. The current and a favourable wind took them swiftly to their destination. Soon the three boys and the archaeologist were among the mighty pylons and obelisks of Karnak. But they did not linger long amid the many columns, nor in the halls of the temple with its colossal statues of the Pharaohs. Father took them into an adjacent area of ruins thickly sown with small blocks of stone light enough for a boy to lift. Some of these had been piled into symmetrical patterns.

"It will be a task of ten or more years to make order here," Megdi's father said. "These stones belonged to a temple that was built more swiftly than all the other temples of Karnak, and that disappeared from the face of the earth with even greater haste. It was completely razed and the stones of it used to erect pylons. But we think we can put the original temple together again."

They sat down in the shade of a few palms which rose above the rubble-strewn field.

180

"When this temple was built," the archaeologist related, "Egypt was a great and widely feared empire. Tribute and gifts poured into Thebes. So rich was she that the Kings of Mitanni and Chatti, or Ashur and Babylon, occasionally begged the Pharaohs, their 'big brothers,' for money. Mercenary armies composed of Asiatics and Africans, auxiliary troops drawn from the peoples of the desert, Shardina with long daggers, round shields and horned helmets, guarded the borders from foes from without and put down any rebellion from within. The third Thutmose was followed by his son Amenophis, a giant of a man famous for possessing a bow that he alone could bend. So incredible was his aim, that, the tale is told, he could stand in a moving war chariot and shoot an arrow through nine copper disks. So great was his strength that when the rowers of his barge were exhausted, the Pharaoh himself took up a pair of oars and all alone rowed the barge to its destination. Amenophis was a mighty war maker, like his father. When he returned home from his first campaign, he drove before him fifty Asiatic princes, together with their wives and children, horses and chariots. Seven slain kings hung from the bow of his ship when he docked at Thebes. The booty he had amassed amounted to one hundred thousand pounds of copper and almost sixteen hundred pounds of gold, as well as vessels and vases of untold magnificence.

"Amenophis was succeeded by the fourth Thutmose, the first excavator in recorded history. It was this Pharaoh, acting on divine command, who dug away the sand that had covered the Great Sphinx by the pyramids of Giza. A memorial tablet still standing between the forepaws of the Sphinx records this deed."

*Ramses II,
with his sons,
storms a Syrian
fortress*

"What do you mean, 'acting on divine command'?" Megdi asked.

"Well, the story is that when still a young prince, Thutmose IV was hunting lions near the pyramids. Overcome by the midday heat, he went to sleep in the shade of the mighty head that towered out of the desert sands. In a dream the Sphinx spoke to him, complained about its condition, and made him promise that he would save it from the encroaching desert. In return, the Sphinx predicted that he would be successor to the throne.

"However, this Pharaoh wore the two crowns only a few years, years of much fighting. But his son, Amenophis III, enjoyed to the full the power and the glory of the New Kingdom. He waged warfare only during the first seven years of his reign. Thereafter Egypt was so unchallenged in her dominance that the Pharaoh could devote himself without hindrance to the pleasures of a ruler's life. He erected buildings as large as whole cities, arranged water festivals and great hunts. He had the outstanding events of his reign inscribed on memorial scarabs, just as later rulers would use memorial coins for that purpose. From one of these scarabs we learn that the king killed fifty-six wild bulls on a single day, and 102 lions in the course of ten years. Near his palace a lake for pleasure-sailing was created. It measured 4,000 by 1,000 feet, and was constructed in a matter of two weeks. The lake was created to satisfy the whim of his wife Tiy, who wished to go sailing in a gold-trimmed barge called 'Radiant as Aten' on the very edge of the desert!

"Tiy is remembered for this extravagance, but she must have been remarkable in other ways. For one thing, not a drop of royal blood flowed in Tiy's veins. She was the daughter of a courtier named Yuya and his wife Tuyu. But although we read of Yuya that he was the king's mouth and ear, the phrase might even better be applied to his daughter, who married the Pharaoh and who, like her parents, was accorded a tomb in the Valley of the Kings. After the death of the Pharaoh, the king of Mitanni wrote to his widow: 'You know all the words which we spoke together; no other knows them.' In other words, she was truly a co-ruler, acquainted with all the affairs of the government. Of course Amenophis had other wives, including the Asiatic princess, Giluchipa, whose hand he requested seven times, and who brought 317 girls into the harem with her. But Tiy alone was considered to be the queen, and it may well be that she was wiser and more far-sighted than the king.

"Tiy bore him a son who was named after him. In the thirtieth year of his father's reign he was raised to the throne as Amenophis IV, in accordance with the practice of the times that when a king felt his strength diminishing, he would share the power with his heir. Shortly afterwards Amenophis III died and his son became sole Pharaoh.

"Amenophis IV was the ninth ruler of the Eighteenth Dynasty. In the fifth year of his reign he declared war on the gods to whom the temples of Thebes had been erected. He stripped the priests, who owned a third of the land, of all their wealth. He then left the splendid capital of the New Kingdom and moved two hundred miles farther north to found a new capital city in a place 'which previously had belonged to no god and no goddess.' He called his new city Akhetten, 'Horizon of Aten.' Putting aside his own name, which meant 'Amen is gracious,' he called himself henceforth

184

Akhenaten, a name more widely known in the form of Ikhnaton. We do not know what prompted him to take this revolutionary step; we can only make guesses. He himself speaks of an 'unprecedented offence' committed against him by the Theban priesthood. There is no question but that the priesthood had risen to such power that the Pharaohs must have had difficulty controlling them. It was the blessing and the secret sign of the supreme god of these priests which decided who was to be Pharaoh—remember the cases of Thutmose III and Hatshepsut. Thus, the supreme god kept check upon the Pharaoh, while a horde of lesser gods kept watch over the doings of the common people.

"The new Pharaoh had grown up with the sons of Asiatic princes, and had received a good education from his energetic mother Tiy and his wise father Amenophis. He appears to have felt that the multitude of gods was as unnecessary as the boundaries between Egypt and other countries. Perhaps he knew something of the machinations of the priests and had seen them produce false miracles in the temples that only too well served their purposes of frightening and hoodwinking the people.

"The young king thirsted after the truth. Besides his new name he assumed a royal title which meant 'Living by the truth.' The faith he wanted to implant in the hearts of all men, not only the Egyptians, was to be clear as the brightness of day, pure as the shining of the sun. All men were to have equal share in the light that poured down from heaven. All men were to learn that the throne of the world was occupied by One Being from whom all glory and all warmth came, who created all life and all beauty. Amenophis IV gave this Being the name of Aten. And he praised

185

Aten

this Supreme Being, who could not be grasped in words or pictures,
in a hymn which has survived the centuries:

> Thou appearest beautifully on the horizon of heaven,
> Thou living Disk, the beginning of life!
> When thou art risen on the Eastern Horizon,
> Thou hast filled every land with thy beauty.
> Thou art gracious, great, glistening, and high over every land;
> Thy rays encompass the lands to the limit of all thou hast made;
> Though thou art far away, thy rays are on earth;
> When thou settest in the Western Horizon,
> The land is in darkness, in the manner of death.
> People sleep in a room, with heads wrapped up,
> Nor sees one eye the other.
> Every lion is come forth from his den;
> All creeping things, they sting.
> At daybreak, when thou arisest on the horizon,
> Thou drivest away the darkness;
> The Two Lands are in festivity every day.
> Awake, men do their work.
> All beasts are content with their pasturage;
> Trees and plants are flourishing.
> The birds which fly from their nests,

186

Their wings are stretched out in praise of thee.
The ships are sailing north and south as well,
For every way is open at thy appearance.
The fish in the river dart before thy face;
Thy rays are in the midst of the great green sea.
Creator of the son in the womb of his mother,
On the day when he is born
Thou openest his mouth completely,
Thou suppliest his necessities.
Thou seest to it that the chick breaks from its shell,
That it cheeps gaily and runs about when it comes from the egg.
Thou hast created men and beasts,
All that goes about on the earth,
The lands of Syria and Nubia, the land of Egypt.
Thou hast given men various tongues.
Thou hast created the Nile, which springs forth from the nether world,
Thou hast placed a Nile in the sky,
That it may water the fields.
Glorious are thy plans, O Lord in eternity!
The Nile from the sky is for foreign lands,
The Nile from the nether world for Egypt.
Thy rays awaken all gardens to life.
Thou makest the seasons, the winter's cold and summer's heat.
Thou hast made millions of forms out of thyself.
In villages and cities, in streets and on streams,
Eyes are raised up to thee, who passes radiant over the earth.
Thou art in my heart; there is none who truly knows thee
Except thy son Ikhnaton.
Thou hast given to him to see
That the world is in thy hand.
Thou art life; every man lives through thee.

Since thou hast created the earth, it is prepared for thy son
Who came forth from thee. . . .

"The hymn is unique in the annals of Egypt for its sincere and reverent manner. Apparently the insights of his new faith made a great poet out of the Pharaoh. He worshipped this one god Aten alone and turned away from the many other gods to whom temples had previously been erected in Egypt. Moreover, he came to the conclusion—equally unusual in a Pharaoh—that his own people were no more important than others; in fact, he placed Syria and Nubia before Egypt in his hymn, in his enumeration of the lands of the earth. His hymn celebrated the unity of earth, of heaven, of God. Earlier Pharaohs had built pyramids of stone or mud bricks; Ikhnaton envisioned a pyramid whose golden apex, the sun, stood high in the sky, its rays reaching down like mighty fingers of a divine hand to the earth and freely giving warmth, radiance, and life. This all-embracing 'pyramid' of light became the symbol of the new religion, and Ikhnaton had this symbol carved and painted in temples and tombs. With impatient ardour he set about building a city for this radiant god. He chose a plain which Aten himself had ringed round with hills, and which was equally distant from Thebes and from the White Walls. Boundary stones for the new city were set up, and Ikhnaton took an oath over these boundary stones never to leave the area of this city. He would honour the god by voluntarily cloistering himself in the god's city. On the barren plain, sealed off by rocky ridges toward the east and bordered by the Nile on the west, there rose up at the king's command great temples connected by bridges with the palaces; shining streets, ined by the houses of the nobles; dockyards along the Nile; and tombs in the eastern mountains. Ikhnaton broke with the old tradition of having eternal dwellings built in the west. He broke with Osiris as well as with Anubis, the first of the Western Ones. As he saw it, the east was the place of the eternal rising. His temples, moreover, were laid out differently from the temples for Amen or Hathor or Min. They were reminiscent of the sun temples which had been erected by the sons of the Sun toward the end of the Old Kingdom.

"In the new city's great temple of Aten, colonnades enclosed a wide courtyard, in the centre of which was placed the altar. Statues of the king stood in the colonnades. Alongside the temple, flanked by walls and avenues of trees, were storehouses and the treasury. Everything imaginable was stored in these buildings: chests and splendid vessels of gold and silver, pitchers, bowls, baskets, bales of linen. A lovely arbour decorated with pennants and golden uraeus snakes stood ready for the king's pleasure.

"The palaces were as spacious as the temples, and the homes of the nobles were proportionately on a magnificent scale. Thus the domain of the supervisor of Aten's herds of cattle was 250 by 230 feet. The extensive outbuildings included stables, storehouses, and ovens for baking. There were spacious living quarters, sleeping chambers for the master of the house, his wives and children, two baths, and a garden which the architect had laid out with particular care. An impressive gate, dignified by turrets, led from an outer court into this garden, which contained a pond surrounded by trees and shrubs. A ramp led up to a small temple. In the course of the excavations, the roots and remains of seventy-six trees and bushes

189

were found. In all likelihood the entire city was one great flowering garden that extended for miles, planted upon soil brought in from the fertile riverbanks to this desert place. There were birdhouses and many ponds for fish. It was like a vast garden of paradise, a wholly new city such as Egypt had never known.

"The people who surrounded Pharaoh were also new. He chose his officials from among men who wholeheartedly accepted his new religion, and showered tributes and gifts upon them. 'He has made them men of gold!' the soldiers and children cried, dancing for joy. Those who subscribed to the new doctrines could rise to the highest ranks, could become fanbearers on Pharaoh's left or right, chief overseers of Ikhnaton's horses, chiefs of police, and generals of the army. The men whom Ikhnaton elevated openly admitted in the inscriptions on their tombs: 'I was nothing by birth; the king made me.' Chief Sculptor Bek testified: 'His Majesty instructed me and made me great.' The vizier Ramose invoked Pharaoh: 'You O Pharaoh, are the Only One of Aten; you hold in your possession all his ordinances. You control the mountains; they tremble in their secret chambers as do the hearts of men with fear of you. The mountains hear you, as the people listen to you.'

"The king himself was the sole priest of Aten; he instructed scribes, architects, sculptors, and officials in the proper manner of worshipping Aten. A General Maya freely admits: 'My lord has promoted me because I listened to his teachings.' Many of these upstarts were foreigners. An Asiatic named Tutu, for example, occupied one of the highest ranks in the kingdom.

"The queen who shared the throne with Ikhnaton, Nefertiti, was an unusual and radiantly beautiful woman. There are many indica-
190

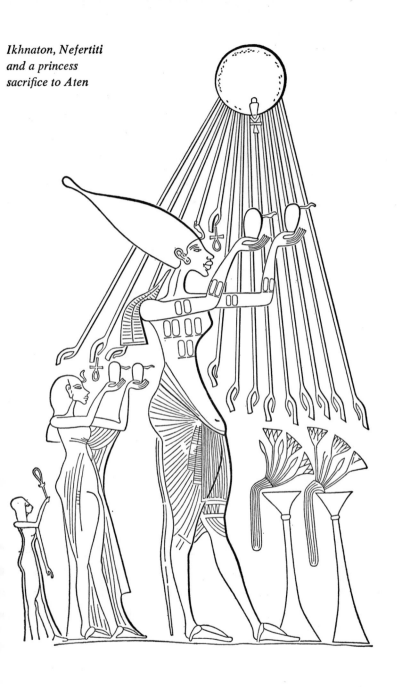

Ikhnaton, Nefertiti and a princess sacrifice to Aten

tions that she was the most ardent advocate of the new religion, and that she stirred up Ikhnaton's hatred of the old gods until at last he went so far as to have tombs broken open in order to have the names of Amen and his brood of lesser gods wiped out even in such hidden places. As a destroyer of the past Ikhnaton exceeded even the depredations of Thutmose III.

"At this point in Ikhnaton's career his mother, Tiy, announced somewhat nervously that she was coming to visit him. She had not moved to Akhetaten with the rest of the court. The Pharaoh hastily built her a palace which he called Shadow of Aten. His mother arrived, and earnestly counselled him to practise moderation. Evidently her words made a considerable impression on the king, for the upshot of this mother-in-law's visit was a quarrel with Nefertiti, who was not prepared to make peace with the foes of her god. She moved into a palace of her own. Subsequently, her name was removed from many places where it had been inscribed. Nefertiti had presented the king with a number of daughters. Now this happy family was broken up. The picture of the king in the midst of his family, a standard motif in the decoration of temples and tombs, no longer corresponded to the truth. Ikhnaton became a lonely man. True, the 'sons of Nobody whom he had raised up out of the dust' continued to flood him with flattery. They expressed the wish that he might 'be happy in his city until the swan turns black and the raven white, until the mountains move and the rivers flow upstream.' But even as they continued to glorify him as 'the god who makes men great, who is the Nile for all of us,' we

Opposite: *The natural pyramid, El Qurn* (above); *The Valley of the Kings* (below)

Ikhnaton's subjects pray to Aten

Opposite: *The Pharaoh Tutankhamen and his wife Ankhesnamen under the rays of Aten*

cannot help but hear the greed and supplication in their voices.

"The portraits of many of these favourites show them as men with rough, rude faces. The sculptors and painters who worked under Ikhnaton followed the king's biddings and treated their subjects realistically. No exception was made for Pharaoh or his family. The artists show Ikhnaton with a long head, protruding ears and thick lips. It may be that in some of their portraits they carried truthfulness further than Pharaoh expected, and showed him and his family with sagging bellies and distorted faces and limbs. It was apparently customary to give royal children small-sized models of the royal chariot. When the Pharaoh went out for a drive, he would himself hold the reins, while his bodyguard ran panting alongside him. But in certain pictures where the royal children are shown riding in their toy chariots, a monkey would be holding the reins and the horses would be rearing up and about to bolt. Covertly that is, there was a tendency to mock the Pharaoh. Worse still, he was deceived. From letters which have come down to us, it is clear that his closest adviser, the Asiatic Tutu, concealed from him events that were happening on Egypt's borders. Aziru, a cunning prince of Syria, evidently had a secret understanding with Tutu, for he seized city after city in Syria, and finally besieged Byblos. Byblos was defended by Ribaddi, who was faithful to Pharaoh. Ribaddi appealed to Ikhnaton for help: 'Behold, Aziru has attacked your garrisons and has imprisoned the envoys whom I sent to Simyra. Both the city of Beruta and the city of Ziuna are assailing me with their warships. All those who can bear arms in the land of the Amorites have gathered against us . . . Give me soldiers!'

"No help came, nor even a reply. Ribaddi wrote again. 'It is bitter

194

for me to relate what evils have come over the lands of the king because of Aziru, that treacherous dog. There is lamentation in our fortress. March against this man of violence and destroy him. This land is your land. And since I have called to you and you have not stirred, Simyra has been lost. We have no money to buy horses. We have been pillaged. Send thirty divisions with horses and chariots and men, men, men—I have nothing more, not so much as a horse!'

"It seems that these appeals for aid never reached Ikhnaton because Tutu was in league with Aziru. Thus it came about that in the end Byblos, too, fell, that the Hittites advanced and the Syrian princes captured one Egyptian province after the other. The Khabiru invaded Egyptian territory. Megiddo, Askalon, and Gezer cried for help. Their appeals went unheard. In vain the deserted provincials reminded the king of Thutmose III, who had made short work of any rebellion. Ikhnaton went on serenely planning new cities for Aten in Asia, and Nubia. Tutu and his other courtiers kept him cut off from the world, with the result that he was even more immersed in his religious doctrines. In the end he became his own prisoner in the desert paradise he had created for his god. But even within the bounds of his own city, sedition was rampant. Thus, in the tomb of a police chief, we find a representation of spies being questioned; a fire is burning in the background, and it is clear that it will be used to make the culprits talk.

"Twelve years after the Pharaoh had overthrown the gods of Thebes and had robbed the priests of their incomes, the offended priests were prepared to strike back. They had a mighty force behind them, for people of the most devious callings had suffered

195

serious economic losses on account of the newfangled religion: amulet makers and amulet dealers, bakers of sacrificial bread and carvers of *ushabtis,* officers and soldiers who could no longer hope for booty on campaigns. Moreover, the populace had a far greater and more deeply rooted faith in Osiris than it had in the newly proclaimed supreme and single deity. The disappointed, the embittered, the ambitious, the lazy, and perhaps some sincere and earnest defenders of the old faith, gathered together to oppose Pharaoh. There was civil war. So formidable was the army that marched against the city of Aten that resistance was impossible. The city was abandoned so hastily that the sculptors left behind their models, the officials their archives of royal letters. The panic-stricken inhabitants did not even take the time to release their dogs from the kennels or their birds from the cages. A terrible revenge was taken on the deserted city. Just as Ikhnaton had destroyed the names and images of the other gods, so now the symbols of Aten were erased from tombs, temples, even quarries. The name which the proscribed Pharaoh had given to himself was banned, could not again be spoken. Henceforth he was referred to only as Khru Akhetaten: the Criminal of Akhetaten. The priests of Thebes announced triumphantly: 'The city of him who transgressed against thee, Amen, has fallen to dust. The sun of him who offended against thee has set!'

"In the tomb of Queen Tiy has been found a sarcophagus bearing traces of the name Ikhnaton and the sign of the new god, though both name and symbol have been almost completely chiselled away. Above the face of the mummy lay a golden vulture, its talons fixed firmly in the mummy's eye sockets. When this was first discovered, it was thought to be the mummy of Ikhnaton. But closer examination made it seem more probable that it was rather the mummy of his successor Semenkhkare, whom Ikhnaton had married to one of his daughters, raised to co-regent, and perhaps on Tiy's advice was planning to use as an intermediary to bring about a reconciliation with the priesthood of Thebes. It seems probable, therefore, that the followers of Amen granted decent burial to Semenkhkare and Tiy, while the body of the heretic king was vengefully destroyed.

"The Horizon of Aten had lasted little more than a decade; then it had collapsed, and with it the remarkable reign of this most amazing of all Pharaohs. Ikhnaton had been destroyed by the contradictions within himself as much as by the hatred of his enemies. He had preached love—and had practised religious persecution. He had raised up the lowly, only to find himself hemmed in by obsequious careerists. He had wanted to be a father to all peoples— and had not helped his people against foreign conquerers. He had proclaimed universal brotherhood, yet how explain the faces of Negroes, Libyans, and Asiatics carved upon the ramp leading up to his palace upon which he symbolically trod."

"A bad king!" Achmed decided firmly. This time, Jacob was of the same mind.

"But didn't you say there are people who think he was a great Pharaoh?" Megdi asked his father.

"A great many people think so," Father said. "And I agree with them."

"Why?" Megdi asked.

"Perhaps I should first admit that Ikhnaton had grave weaknesses," Father said. "But he was perhaps the first person in recorded history who tried to open the eyes of others to the fact that

197

men are brothers to one another. He was also the first who tried to free men from the domination of cunning priests who heaped up vast treasures in their temples. But he was a voice crying in the wilderness. Because he himself was not free of error, but above all because neither the Egyptians nor other peoples understood him, he was destroyed. He was in advance of his times, but his influence continued to be felt, far more strongly than that of a Thutmose or a Ramses, say, who had made other nations as well as the Eygptians tremble in fear. Ikhnaton's hymn to the sun scattered seed that sprouted and bore much fruit. In a papyrus dating from many centuries after his time we find the words: 'You ask who are they who lead us to the heavenly kingdom? The birds of the air and all the beasts below and upon the earth, the fishes of the sea, they are those who lead us, and the heavenly kingdom is within us.' Such words go back to Ikhnaton who proclaimed the sacredness of the lower forms of life and the unity of all creation. Perhaps he lacked the qualities of a successful ruler, but he belongs among the great teachers of mankind."

Jacob looked thoughtfully down at the ground. He was a Copt, and many elements in Ikhnaton's hymn to the sun had reminded him of words in his Holy Book. But Achmed had, apparently, some hard and fast standards by which he judged those long-dead rulers of Egypt.

"He let himself be deceived and fooled by his advisers," Achmed said. "Anyone who does that isn't going to amount to much."

Father smiled at the incisiveness of the boy's mind. "You are right there, Achmed," he said.

They had to row back across the Nile. The current was against them. Megdi, Achmed, and Jacob took turns at the oars, while
198

Megdi's father held the rudder. "I still owe you a story," he said suddenly. "I haven't yet told you how the city of the heretic Pharaoh was discovered. It began with a peasant woman who was digging for saltpetre and came upon inscribed clay tablets. She filled a sack with the peculiar tablets and took them to a dealer. By the time she reached town, most of the tablets had turned to dust in the sack. The few that remained intact were sent to Paris, but were dismissed by scholars as worthless stuff. But some German excavators heard of the tablets, came to Akhetaten, which is now called Tel el Amarna, and looked around carefully. They discovered some three hundred letters from Asiatic kings inscribed on clay tablets in cunei-form script—that is the writing in wedge-shaped signs which was used by the ancient Babylonians. When they had completed the decipherment of these tablets, they knew that they had stumbled upon Ikhnaton's royal archives.

"Fifteen years later Sir Flinders Petrie found some remains of temples to Aten and of the workers' barracks. These were some-what on the outskirts of Akhetaten, not far from the place which had once been the greatest alabaster quarry in all of Egypt. This quarry was called Hatnub, which meant House of Gold. Today there is an enormous crater there, like something dug by a falling meteorite; it is 330 feet across at the top. The ancient Egyptians had taken their alabaster from there since at least the time of Cheops. The workers' quarters that Petrie found consisted of wretched little houses. In 1911 a German archaeologist named Ludwig Borchardt discovered the workshop of the best sculptor of the new city. Wonderful sculptures were found amid the rubble, including that bust of Nefertiti which has become world famous.

"The English archaeologist Sir Charles Leonard Woolley dug for some time in Tel el Amarna, but found nothing more significant than a few fragments of walls. Then he came upon two stone cylinders which had once been part of pillars, no doubt temple pillars. It was obvious that the temple itself, like many other great buildings of antiquity, had been dismembered for its stone. But from traces in the mortar which covered the foundations Woolley was able to deduce the size and shape of the stone blocks making up the walls. And when the mortar was removed, fine red lines appeared: the architect's plan, marked out with string which had been dipped in red paint. Bits of wood were found in holes which had been dug deep into the ground. These bits were the last remains of great flagpoles which had once stood in front of the temple gate. One clue after the other was found, until at last the excavators were able to reconstruct the temple of which scarcely a stone remained. In time the whole city of Aten could be visualized, conjured out of its ruins anew, as Ikhnaton had raised it up out of nothingness.

"When Woolley carefully examined the workers' quarters, he discovered that the houses were all exactly alike. A single house differed from the others in not having its door fronting on the street; it presented a blank back to the row of houses opposite it. Evidently the man who lived in that house had quarrelled with his neighbours. Since he could not move, being bound to his place of work, he simply turned his house around. Evidently Ikhnaton's city was not a paradise for everybody in it.

"To this day quarrelling and hatred flourish on the soil of Tel el Amarna. There have been feuds between the villages of Till and Hagg Kandil from time immemorial. Sometimes their quarrels have led to bloody vendettas. These have had repercussions for archaeology. In 1912 the people of Hagg Kandil destroyed overnight the most beautiful floor of Aten's city, a floor that had been uncovered only after months of toil. They did this because the gaffers who were guarding it were men of Till."

"They destroyed the whole floor?" Megdi asked incredulously.

"The entire thing," Father said.

"But what was the sense of that?" Megdi cried indignantly. "I never heard of anything so stupid."

"It made sense," Achmed said with sullen satisfaction. It was clear that he could enter into the native point of view better than Megdi's father could.

"But what had the archaeologists to do with the feud?" Megdi demanded.

"They hired the men of Till, didn't they? They gave the men of Till money," Achmed countered. "Besides, they carried away the things they found, and the people who owned the land had nothing for it—as usual."

"A pity that Gurgar is not here," Father commented. "Gurgar knows better than anyone else who went empty-handed and who did not when the great finds in Egypt were made."

"One thing is sure, old Gurgar has gone empty-handed every time," Achmed asserted. "And yet he was the discoverer of the most famous tomb in this country—or wasn't he?" he asked, for the archaeologist's smile made him a little uncertain.

"Ask him yourself," Father advised.

At Sheik Ali's house a telegram was waiting for the archaeologist.

"We must go back to Cairo," Father said after he had read it.

"When?" Megdi asked anxiously. "Not tomorrow!"

"Tomorrow by the night train," Father replied. "But we will still have all day for Biban el Muluk."

IN THE VALLEY OF SILENCE

The following morning Gurgar and the three boys ascended the same path they had taken the day before. But this time Gurgar did not stop at the half-way point; he continued to lead the way on up. The gorge of Dai al-Bahri, the mortuary temple on the rim of the valley, the Nile, the green strips on either shore, the whole living world, it seemed, was left behind them. Megdi felt as if he had suddenly set foot upon another planet. He looked about him—there was not a blade of grass or a weed, nothing but naked rock. He looked for a bird—the sky was empty. On the left the peak shaped like a pyramid rose starkly towards the sun, and on the right the valley opened out like some lunar crater. Amazingly, however, there was a highway leading into this valley, and smaller roads down below as well. Megdi stared, fascinated, at the black doorways in the cliff walls to which each of these roads led. Never had he seen such forbidding entrances. They looked as if there was no emerging from their dark bowels.

Gurgar had stopped at last. "Biban el Muluk," he said, pointing. "The Valley of the Kings. This valley has witnessed more glory and more wretchedness, more greatness and misery, more grand adventures and terrible disappointments, than any other valley in Egypt, perhaps than any other in the whole world."

"There," Achmed exclaimed excitedly, pointing to a doorway into the rock, bounded by a wall, lying immediately below another. "There is the tomb that Gurgar discovered. There were more treasures in that tomb than in any other tomb in Egypt. But what did Gurgar get out of it?"

"It seems you know more about it than I do," Gurgar answered mockingly. "As it happens, I neither came away empty-handed, nor was I the discoverer."

Achmed grew heated. "Everybody knows that *you* found the first step, and that you did not get an ounce of the gold that was found. And yet the gold coffin alone weighed more than 450 pounds. There were four chambers filled with treasures—and the man who found the way into them received nothing. Others took the glory and the riches for themselves!"

"How old are you, anyway?" Gurgar asked in an offhand tone.

"Fourteen," Achmed said, taken aback by the question.

"That surprises me," Gurgar commented. "The only people I've ever heard talk such silly nonsense up to now are the old men of Qurna—none of whom were there, of course. I was on the spot, you know. And if you really want to hear the true story I could tell you pretty well who came off empty-handed and who did not."

Achmed looked a little abashed. He would have preferred to keep his version of the affair. Gurgar led the boys off to one side of the path which descended into the valley. They came to a great flat rock, like a huge table, and here they sat down. "No one will disturb us here," Gurgar said. He gazed for a moment over the valley, his eyes passing from tomb to tomb. More intensely than ever, the boys felt the silence that brooded over the barren terrain.

"The later kings," Gurgar began, speaking in a muted voice as though under the spell of the uncanny stillness, "sought out this valley of silence and appointed it their resting place. The first was Thutmose, the father of Queen Hatshepsut. Why did he decide to have his eternal dwelling built here? Earlier kings had built pyramids, as you know. But all the pyramids, no matter whether they had been made of mud bricks or granite blocks, had been broken open and pillaged. It was probably King Thutmose's chief architect, a man named Ineni, who persuaded the Pharaoh to establish his eternal dwelling in this bleak sun-scorched valley, beneath a pyramid which had 'stood from the very beginning of the world.' At any rate, in Ineni's tomb we find the inscription: 'I alone was there when the Sublime One's dwelling was hewn out of the rock. No one else saw it, no one heard it.' Of course this does not mean that so eminent a man as the chief architect wielded hammer and chisel and cut the tomb with his own hands. There was a team of workmen to do that. But they did not count—and perhaps they were done away with, afterwards, to keep the secret the more secure.

"The passage that was cut for the first Thutmose was not especially deep. The tombs of later kings had shafts twice, three times, even five times as deep. The reason for this was certainly not only concern about robbers, but also to make the tombs as grand as possible. The reliefs, paintings, and inscriptions on the walls of the underground corridors and chambers revealed the true secrets of the kings, the mysteries of their religion.

204

"But now let us talk about those who did not depart empty-handed." Gurgar threw a sharp look at Achmed. "Those daring fellows who in all ages descended upon the valley and desecrated its silence. The first of these came while the Pharaohs were still reigning.

"By a strange trick of fate, we possess a document bearing on the earliest grave robberies. It is a document which might have easily gone astray. This is what happened: about a hundred years ago half of a papyrus scroll was brought to Europe. It contained an account of the trial of grave robbers. But the story did not really make sense, since the first half was missing. Then, one day in February, 1935, a Belgian archaeologist found a papyrus scroll concealed inside a hollow wooden statue. Unfolding it just a little with the tip of his knife, he began reading. The date alone startled him. It was the year 16 of the reign of Ramses IX. Once the beginning of the scroll had been deciphered, the scholar realized that he had in his hands the missing half of the grave robber story. The whole tale ran something like this: Pesiur, the Mayor of Thebes, had charged his personal enemy, Pevero, who was responsible for the security of graves, with having allowed the tombs of kings and queens to be desecrated. An investigating commission looked into the matter and discovered that most of the tombs were unharmed. But one royal tomb, that of Sebekemsaf, had been broken into. The pillagers had dug a corridor and stolen the king's mummy.

"On orders from the vizier, the chief suspect, a coppersmith named Pekhor, was led blindfolded to the site of the crime. There the blindfold was removed. Threatened with torture, he went up to a tomb which was just being built and declared under oath that he

205

never set foot in any tomb but this one. Pevero felt that he had won this bout. So, too, did the court which had been quickly convened, but as the investigation proceeded, other things came to light which were by no means to Pevero's credit. It seemed that serious crimes had been committed during his term of office. A certain Amenpnufer confessed in court that he, together with a stonemason named Haspver, had been making a regular practice of plundering tombs. From the year 13 of the reign of Ramses IX, he had collaborated with the carpenter Setnakht, the decorator Hapio, the agricultural worker Amenemhab, the water carrier Khaemvese, and the boatman of the mayor of Thebes in robbing royal graves; these yielded far greater profits than the tombs of the nobles, on which they had used to prey. Amenpnufer made a detailed confession: 'With copper chisels we cut a passage through the rough masonry with which the corridors were blocked. We found the king, this god, and his wife, and we opened the sarcophagi. The noble mummy was covered over and over with gold, and his coffins were of silver and gold and precious stones. We took from this god all the gold, and also took other things, gold and silver and copper utensils, and brought them across the river. What we left behind, we set fire to. But after a few days the chief overseer of the graves had me taken prisoner. Then I gave the scribe of that quarter of the city my share of the booty, and he let me go, and I received from my comrades once again what was coming to me. There are many others who do as we did. . . . '

"This episode took place at the time of the Twentieth Dynasty. It is hard for us, today, to realize the full magnitude of the crime involved. For the robbers were risking not only torture and painful death but, even if they were not caught, they were running foul of the curse which the priests had placed upon the royal graves when they sealed them. 'I have set ablaze all the area around me; the flames will seize any man who approaches me with hostile intent,' was one of the many spells. Mersegret, the snake goddess, was lurking in the tomb, ready to sink her deadly fangs into any grave robber. Nevertheless, the robberies continued. The plunderers were mostly workers and artisans of the necropolis. Irresistibly drawn by the glitter of gold, time and again these men broke into the tombs of the Pharaohs and made away with precious funerary gifts and coffins. Undoubtedly many of the plunderers found willing accomplices among the guards. Without this, it would have been scarcely conceivable for them to escape the numerous pitfalls of the tombs and pierce through stone obstacles many yards thick. It was a highly organized conspiracy, and even priests in charge of the dead were involved in it.

"However, not all of the priests were corrupt and cynical. A small band of loyal priests had vowed to save at least the mummies from the robbers, if they could not save the gold coffins and amulets. Under the cloak of night, with a secrecy that would have befitted criminals, these priests would visit the plundered tombs and carry away the desecrated bodies of their kings to new hiding places. Three times Ramses III was moved. Finally no less than thirteen royal mummies had been collected in the tomb of Amenophis II, the king of the legendary bow. And a total of thirty-six royal mummies, with their stone sarcophagi, were transported to a hiding place in the cliff above the temple of Dai al-Bahri. They were moved in the dead of night, over a difficult path across the

207

barren ridges, and for once the secret remained safe. For three thousand years they lay there untouched. Only in recent days were they disturbed—for the guild of grave robbers outlived all the dynasties of the Pharaohs."

"Not bad," Achmed said with a certain satisfaction.

"It is nothing to be proud of," Gurgar snapped. "In the year 1871 a certain Ali Abderrasul, a native of Qurna, together with his brother Mohammed and a man of another clan, were engaged in some private digging when they came upon a walled-up shaft which led to the hiding place of the mummies. The men took up their pickaxes and soon broke through the wall. Ali Abderrasul had himself lowered on a rope into the black depths of the shaft. He made his way through a horizontal passage to a chamber. He saw a host of sarcophagi massed together. With the mentality of an experienced grave robber, he instantly decided that this fantastic find was for himself and his brother. The third man must be kept out of it. And so he pelted back through the passage, uttering cries of terror, and had himself hauled back up in a hurry. An afreet, an evil spirit, dwelt down there, he babbled. The three fled. But later the two brothers returned in the dead of night with a donkey they had killed, and threw it down into the pit, to produce the foul smell by which evil spirits are recognized. Things turned out to their gratification; the stench was fearful and everyone had a proper dread of the shaft. No one dared go near. But members of the Abderrasul clan, bound by a vow of silence, methodically drew upon the treasures of the dead kings. There was enough treasure in the hiding place to assure a livelihood for even so large a clan as Abderrasul's for many generations.

Opposite: *The golden mask of Tutankhamen*

"But the clan was not to keep its private gold mine. About ten years after the discovery, the head of the Cairo museum, an excellent scholar named Maspero, began to wonder at the way more and more Egyptian funerary gifts of priceless value and mysterious origin kept turning up in collections in Europe and America. Maspero set a young assistant of his to track down the robbers. Various clues pointed to Qurna. Finally this amateur detective became certain that all the threads led to two men: a person named Mustafa Aga Ayat, who held the threefold post of British, Russian, and Belgian consul in Luxor; and Ali Abderrasul. Since Mustafa Aga Ayat had diplomatic immunity, the assistant had Ali Abderrasul arrested. Ali was questioned. He denied that he knew anything. He was impervious to threats, attempts at bribery, even torture. Finally, after two months he was released. He went to the triple consul and showed him the traces of the torture on his feet. On the strength of this, he demanded a large share—until now he had been content with a fifth of the sales price of the antiquities. Now he wanted half. The consul refused. A bitter quarrel ensued. Finally the thirst for revenge was greater than prudence. Mohammed Abderrasul, Ali's brother, wanted to strike at the consul, and so he went to the mudir and told everything. A telegram was sent to Cairo. Emil Brugsch, brother of the great scholar who as a schoolboy had written a grammar of demotic, at once set out for Qurna. He descended into the shaft—and found himself confronted with an array of Pharaohs such as no archaeologist had ever dreamed would fall to his lot. He began at once salvaging everything the grave robbers had left—and that was a great deal. The mummies lay in the stone sarcophagi which had once enclosed the golden coffins. Within two days Brugsch, aided by a crew of two hundred workmen, had cleared out the hiding place. Forty-eight hours of unsparing toil sufficed him to remove everything from the shaft and bring the whole load down to the Nile. Each sarcophagus had to be carried by twelve or even sixteen men.

"Three days later a steamer carried the mummies of the kings downstream. And something took place that no one could have anticipated. All the way from Thebes to Coptos the fellahin came in droves to the Nile. Men fired off guns, women dashed sand into their faces and raised the same shrill cry of lamentation that thousands of years before had accompanied Pharaohs to their graves. Some people think that this was a tribute from Egypt, perhaps her last, to her kings of the great days of long ago. Be that as it may, the shots and wailing were equally a protest against the foreigners who were taking away thirty-six royal mummies, for all that these were going no farther than the Cairo museum. The local people felt that they were being cheated out of fabulous quantities of gold and other treasures which could be turned into money.

"Ever since archaeologists have appeared on the scene, the robbers have found themselves far more hampered than they ever were by the policemen or soldiers who were occasionally set on their trail. The police and the soldiers could be prevailed on not to see too much. But the scientists were altogether unreasonable. There was no understanding their motives or their conduct. They worked sometimes at the risk of their lives, only to give up everything they had discovered. This made no sense at all to the natives, who had a simple, obvious goal in view."

"They even had fights," Achmed said with satisfaction.

"Hundreds of them," Gurgar agreed. "Let me tell you about just one which is typical. The archaeologist was Howard Carter. He had been working under Petrie and Davis and other famous excavators for more than twenty years, so we can assume he knew a good deal about Egyptian conditions. He had already made a number of amazing finds in the Valley of the Kings. For years he had been chief inspector of excavations in Upper Egypt and Nubia. Now, in 1916, he was spending a few weeks in Luxor, purely on vacation. One day some men from Qurna who had participated in various expeditions with him sought him out. They were highly excited. A regular battle was going on, they said, between two robber bands among the cliffs above the Valley of the Kings. The shooting could be heard in Qurna. This could only mean that someone had made a find important enough to warrant an attack by a rival band. The days in which the evil smell of an afreet would fend off potential enemies were gone forever. The First World War was raging; the happy days of superstition were over, and simple force was the rule.

"Carter decided that there was not a moment to spare. Accompanied by a few men equipped with good lamps and strong ropes, he set out. By the time the little band reached the area, one of the robber bands had already been driven off. The other was busy possessing itself of the find. Carter surprised two men guarding a rope which led down into the newly discovered shaft. The guards fled when they recognized the archaeologist. However, Carter could hear a group of men at work down in the shaft, with no knowledge, evidently, of his arrival. Without more ado he cut the robbers' rope. Then, using his own rope, he descended into the shaft. The hour was just midnight. There were a few tense moments when Carter suddenly confronted the eight tough men who were digging with all their might. He was well aware that these were characters who would stop at nothing. But he knew enough about Egypt and Egyptians to be quite persuasive. In the first place he made it quite clear to them that they were caught in a trap. He offered them a simple choice: they could use his rope, and clear out and nothing more would be said about the matter; or, they could stay where they were without a rope, until the proper authorities were called. The robbers took the more attractive alternative.

"Carter spent the rest of the night on the site. He set about at once investigating the chamber that the grave robbers had invaded. He found a stone sarcophagus, and nothing more. This sarcophagus had not been broken open, but it was empty. On closer examination it turned out that this chamber was one of the two tombs that Hatshepsut had prepared for herself.

"The robbers came off empty-handed. But, you may say, was that not also true for the archaeologist? Not at all. To him that sarcophagus of crystalline sandstone, which had not the slightest value to the pillagers, represented an important discovery. It threw new light on the great queen. This modest tomb outside the Valley of the Kings proved conclusively that Hatshepsut had not been from the beginning the wife of the god and the Pharaoh in one person. She had become sole ruler only at the time she began building her garden of Punt in Dai al-Bahri, and had a tomb prepared in the Val-

Tutankhamen's seal

ley of the Kings which was hewn deeper into the rock than any other royal grave. Carter had a part in the finding of this tomb also. But his great hour struck when he discovered the tomb of the young king—the one you know as 'the Golden Pharaoh'—Tutankhamen."

THE GREAT DISCOVERY

"Then it was Carter who discovered the tomb, not you?" Achmed asked dubiously.

"The discovery belongs to him and to an English lord who paid the costs of the expedition," Gurgar said. "Surely some of the credit should go to the backer. We others helped Carter as well as we could. But the decisive act depended upon him, him alone."

"But Father said that you found the step, all by yourself!"

"What does that matter?" Gurgar said. "The day before, he had pointed out exactly where we were to dig. But let me tell it from the beginning. If ever a discovery in the Valley of the Kings showed what real excavating is, it was Carter's find. Carter, as it happens, was an excellent draughtsman. Even as a young man he had begun copying sketches for an Egyptologist. He did so well that the scholar took him along on his next expedition to the Land of the Pharaohs. Carter helped at excavations conducted by such eminent archaeologists as Davis and Arthur Weigall. He was present when the tombs of Thutmose IV, of Yuya and Tuyu, and of Tiy, were discovered. And in 1907, when the fifth Earl of Carnarvon secured a

214

franchise for excavations in Egypt, Carter was chosen to head the work.

"Digging in the Valley of the Kings had been going on for many years. Davis, for example, had gone over the terrain for twelve years, and had finally come to the conclusion that nothing new could be found there. Maspero, too, thought that the valley was exhausted. By the time Lord Carnarvon and Carter began, the valley had been combed over with a fine-tooth comb. Everywhere mounds of sand and rubble proclaimed: this area has been dug. But there were no maps or drawings which could be relied on. Carter drew up a map. He divided the valley into sharply defined segments, and checked off each field in turn as it was excavated. But in spite of his systematic approach, he worked on and on until 1922, without coming upon anything of great importance.

"In the summer of that year Lord Carnarvon invited the archaeologist to his country house in England. He thanked Carter for his devoted labours, but confessed that he had given up hope of finding anything. Carter appealed to his map. There still remained a sizeable triangle from which rubble and sand had not yet been removed down to bedrock. This area was in the vicinity of the famous tomb of Ramses VI. Carter reminded Lord Carnarvon of the four discoveries which had strengthened his conviction that some day they would come upon the tomb of Tutankhamen, the young king who had reigned after Ikhnaton. These were: some small wafers of gold, a few clay seals, clay vessels, and a cup with the king's name. Finally Lord Carnarvon took courage again and authorized the work to go on. Carter could make one last attempt. That autumn Carter went back to Egypt. He arrived in Luxor on October 28.

215

Seal of the necropolis

Nine days later he telegraphed Lord Carnarvon that he had discovered a tomb with unbroken seals."

"How did it happen?" Megdi asked eagerly.

"It was very simple," Gurgar continued. "Do you see those two black rectangles down there, one right above the other? The upper one is the entrance to the tomb of Ramses VI. We had dug twice right below it, because the road had to be left open for visitors, and because we did not want to destroy the remains of workmen's huts which still stood there from the time of Ramses. Now, however, Carter decided that there was nothing for it but to sacrifice the huts. On November 3, we began tearing down the foundation walls. On the morning of the following day, as we were removing the rubble of the first hut, we suddenly came upon a step in the rock. We sent a boy to call Carter. He came at once. It was very quiet when he arrived. From this moment on he supervised every stroke of the shovels. We worked until it began to grow dark. By then we had twelve steps cleared—and the upper edge of a door on which appeared the unbroken seal of the necropolis: the jackal with twelve prisoners. With shaking hands Carter broke open a hole in the door. He flashed a light into the passage behind the door.

216

The passage was filled with stones—a good sign. Carter had the tomb covered over again, and my friend Hussein and I guarded it through the night. Carter rode away to send a telegram to Lord Carnarvon. The lord and his daughter arrived in Luxor on November 23. The following day the entire staircase was exposed. On the lower part of the door were the seals of Tutankhamen. But why were there two different seals, Carter wondered. He examined the seals more closely—and made a bitter discovery. The tomb had been sealed twice, because robbers had broken in.

"The work continued. The door was opened and the passage behind it cleared. By November 29, Carter had penetrated to a second door. It, too, was sealed with two different seals; it too had been broken through at some time in the distant past. Carter made a small hole. He poked an iron rod through and encountered nothing but air. He flashed his light through the hole and peered into the chamber. Lord Carnarvon, his daughter, and the archaeologist Callender stood in the passage. We can well imagine their suspense.

" 'Can you see anything?' Lord Carnarvon asked.

" 'Yes,' Carter said, 'I see wonders.'

"As his eyes grew accustomed to the dim light, Carter made out a golden chair, golden biers, carriages, statues, alabaster vases, shrines, lamps—an incredible tumbled confusion of precious objects. There was a third door, likewise sealed. Weeks passed before this door could be opened. First the wealth of wonderful objects had to be cleared away without damaging them: couches gleaming with gold, decorated with heads of lions, cows, and hippopotamuses; golden bows and rods; chests and statues. In front of the door stood two life-size guardians of wood, black with golden jewellery, the

217

royal serpent on their foreheads and the herald's staff in their hands. They were surely intended as sentinels in front of the burial chamber, Carter thought. But before he broke open the third sealed door, he made a further discovery. From the antechamber a fourth sealed door led to a side chamber. There was a hole in this door, unmistakably made by robbers. A glance into the chamber confirmed his suspicion, for everything inside was in an incredible jumble. It was obvious that robbers had penetrated into the tomb. But the goddess on the peak of the West had struck without warning, as the ancients would have put it; the criminals had been singed by the flames with which they were theoretically threatened. To put the matter in more realistic terms, the robbers had been caught in the act by incorruptible guards, and presumably marched off to their punishment. In the greatest haste, perhaps deeply ashamed because they had not been alert enough, the responsible officials had sealed the violated tomb anew. They had not taken the time to clean up the mess that the robbers had left. Carter did not mind this so much. But what seriously disturbed him was his observation that the third door too, in front of which the wooden guards had stood for thousands of years, had also been broken open and then closed again. Still, the presence of the seals gave him some cause for hope

"Meanwhile, news of the discovery spread like wildfire. All over the world newspapers carried banner headlines. Hordes of visitors from dozens of countries hastened to the Valley of the Kings. The road that led to the valley was blocked by cars, camels, and donkeys carrying the curious. In order to protect the tomb from the correspondents who came by the score and all of whom assumed the right to enter and look around, Lord Carnarvon gave single newspaper the sole rights of reporting on the find. This brought the wrath of all the other papers down on his head. For months the tomb resembled a beleaguered fortress. But scientific aid came also: the archaeologists Winlock, Mace, Alan Gardiner and James Henry Breasted; the draughtsmen Hauser and Harry Hall; the photographer Burton. Botanists, chemists, an anatomist, also assisted. Every object, no matter how tiny, was recorded on photographic plates, drawing paper, and filing cards. The neighbouring tomb of Seti II served the team as a laboratory. Involved techniques had to be used to forestall the disintegration of woods, fabrics, feathers, and paints. Only by slow, careful work could the utmost value be extracted from this unique find. From a small bouquet of flowers found on a threshold in the tomb the botanist was able to determine that Tutankhamen had been buried at a time when cornflowers and mandrakes were blooming, that is, between the middle of March and the end of April. Carter took three full weeks to reach the bottom of a filled chest painted with magnificent hunting scenes. The antechamber alone contained some seven hundred individual objects.

"Along with this rigorous detail work, every day brought a new quarrel with travel agencies, newspapermen, and all kinds of businessmen with schemes to make profit out of the sensational find.

"At last, on February 17, 1923, the time had come. The contents of the antechamber had been dealt with and the third sealed door could be opened. Some twenty invited guests, scholars and members of the government, took their seats on chairs that had been placed in the antechamber. There was breathless silence as Carter began opening the sealed doors. I was there, to receive the

stones as he prized them loose. After some ten minutes of work th
opening was as wide as two hands. Carter took a flashlight an
peered into the room behind the door. He saw a wall of gold! I
was so close to him that he could touch it by extending his arm ful
length. He prized out more stones. Now the invited guests could als
see the golden wall. When the door stood open at last, the archae
ologists realized that the golden wall was in fact the great shrin
which must contain the sarcophagus. They had often seen suc
shrines depicted on the walls of tombs, but had never before en
countered one in reality. In intense excitement, Carter and Lor
Carnarvon entered the chamber. There was only a narrow corrido
around the golden shrine, and it was blocked by funerary gifts. Thi
shrine was more than sixteen feet long; over ten feet wide, and
nine feet high. It was completely covered with gold beautifully en
graved with figures and texts. After the guests had also examine
the shrine, Carter proceeded to open it, for it was not sealed. H
pushed the bolt back. Creaking, the doors opened. A second gol
shrine appeared, and on its door was a seal. This, then, had neve
been violated. Carter gave a sigh of relief. As quietly as possible
Carter closed the door again. He knew now that the young kin
would be found in the sarcophagus. It would be a pity to break th
seal hastily.

"Before he left the burial chamber, he made a further discovery
In the east wall, opposite the door of the great shrine, was an un
closed door. The chamber to which this door led was likewis
full of wonders. There was a gold triumphal chariot, a shrin
guarded by golden goddesses, a great statue of the god Anubis—
treasure upon treasure. But what were those compared to the cer

inty that the golden shrine which held the mummy of the king ad not been violated. For the first time in the history of Egyptian rchaeology Carter had come to a door untouched by any robber's and. When he left the tomb, the valley itself seemed changed to im, bathed in a special light. He had been granted a victory beond his wildest dreams.

"That victory was dearly bought. In March there were disagreeents between Carter and Lord Carnarvon. Carnarvon insisted at a part of the objects discovered belonged to him. Carter disgreed; he maintained that such an unprecedented find must reain undivided, that neither he nor the lord had the slightest claim o any of it. Then, in April, Lord Carnarvon died, and so Carter

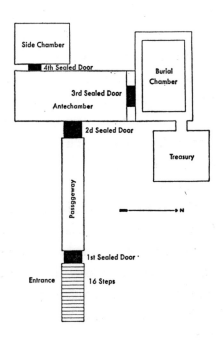

an of Tutankhamen's tomb

lost the friendship and support which had sustained him through those long years of unavailing search and helped him through the turmoil of the last six months. He worked on alone. The principal shrine contained three others, each covered with gold, engraved with incredible delicacy, and each shrine artfully fitted into the other. In eighty-four days of wearisome labour the eighty parts of the shrines, which were clumsy, heavy, and extremely susceptible to damage, were brought out of the tomb.

"The third shrine had been tied with string. Carter cut through it, removed the seal, drew back the bolts—and a fourth shrine appeared. Only after the doors of this fourth shrine had been opened did he at last see the quartzite sarcophagus reflecting the glittering gold of the innermost shrine. Protectively, a goddess figure spread her wings. A massive granite slab formed the cover of the sarcophagus. Inside it—that was now beyond a doubt—Tutankhamen had rested for 3,300 years. The great moment in which the discoverer would be privileged to look into the young king's face was impending, or so it seemed.

"At this point disputes broke out between the Egyptian government and the Carnarvon family. Carter's work was seriously hindered by senseless regulations imposed by the government. Moreover, official quarters took it upon themselves to conduct a stream of visitors to the tomb, in which the larger objects still remained. Carter tried to defend himself. Then the government did something that no one will ever understand: it ordered Carter out of the tomb and forbade him to enter it in the future. Carter filed suit against the government of Egypt. The verdict was against him. The government threw a grand celebration in honour of its court victory. Hun-

222

reds of officials came to the Valley of the Kings. The rocks resounded with speeches denouncing the 'foreigners and intruders,' and fancy fireworks shot into the air!"

Gurgar fell silent. He stared down at the dark rectangles in the valley. "That was an evil day," he murmured, "a day more bitter than any other day in my life. And if it was so bad for me, how it must have hurt *him*. None of us knew where he was. Close to the entrance to the tomb lay his tools, all piled in one heap. We had quickly rescued them from the tomb before the noisy stream of visitors began. Hussein and I stood guard over them, and I assure you, if anyone had tried to touch those tools, we would have fallen on him like watchdogs. That was an evil day for Hussein and me, for Gad Hassan, Awad Achmed, and all those of us who could appreciate what these 'foreigners' had done for Egypt. We could not bear to look on at the way our own people were behaving. An evil day!" Gurgar waved his bony hand through the air as if to drive away a ghost. "Well," he went on with a fierce smile, "hatred and stupidity did not hold the upper hand for good. In any case, who else was there who could have completed so enormous and complicated a job? Afterwards Carter was asked to return, and in February 1926 the anteroom was again filled with his invited guests. The enormously heavy granite lid of the sarcophagus was raised by means of winches. A second coffin appeared underneath. It was difficult to free it from the outer one, since the walls were scarcely a finger's breadth apart and the space between was filled with ointment which in the course of thousands of years had become hard as cement. First, however, the cloth wrappings covering the second coffin were removed, and we saw the incredi-

223

ble golden image of Tutankhamen. The face was of pure gold, th
eyes, eyebrows, and eyelids of aragonite, obsidian, and blue glas
That golden face was rigid, and yet incredibly alive. On the che
of the image, between the crossed hands which held a crook an
fan—the symbols of royal power—there lay a small wreath of flow
ers. There could be scarcely any doubt that the young queen ha
placed it there as a last farewell offering. All of us stood in silenc
looking down on those flowers that had been picked thousands o
years ago.

"With infinite pains, the second coffin was freed from the ston
sarcophagus. Its weight was amazing—for it was of solid gold
A priceless weight of gold enclosed the king's body. Abov
his face, moreover, lay a heavy gold mask, inlaid with lapis lazul
Each of his fingers and toes were protected by gold casing
Around his neck were strings of gems. In the bandages wrappin
the mummy were found more than one hundred groups of golde
amulets, rings, and ornamental disks with inscriptions in which th
gods of heaven and earth greeted the young king: 'Come, O be
loved son, and take the throne of Osiris. Your nobility is perfec
your purity a mirror to the people, your name a shield to you
loved ones, O Tutankhamen, O Osiris, you who are radiant a
Aten.'

"On November 11, 1926, four years after the discovery of th
first step and a full twelve years after the beginning of the searcl
the golden mask was lifted from the Pharaoh's face. The anatomis
made a first incision in the bandages, which had been much eate
by too lavish use of ointment. Carter looked into the face o
Tutankhamen."

Opposite: *Osiris; tomb of Queen Neferti*

Gurgar paused, as though reliving that moment. "I too saw it," he said, "the face of a king too young to be a Living Horus on earth and rule a great empire. Even the golden mask was less moving than the sight of those noble features." Gurgar stood up. "He is still down there," he said. "The only one of all the Pharaohs to remain in the valley. His discoverer insisted that he should not be taken from his tomb. Come. He is waiting for us!"

Gurgar led the way. The descent into the valley was easy and pleasant. The gaffers at the tomb instantly recognized Gurgar and saluted him. Gurgar led the boys down the sixteen steps, through the empty corridor and the barren antechamber, into the inner burial chamber. It seemed small to the boys. They scarcely observed the paintings on the walls. In silence they looked down at the sarcophagus. Achmed, who was surreptitiously watching Gurgar, noticed in amazement that the old man leaned forward in a listening attitude, as if anxious not to miss a word that someone was saying. . . . Perhaps he is talking with the young king, Achmed suddenly thought. And at that moment Gurgar looked at him and nodded.

When they were outside in the sunlight again, the old man pointed to the tomb of Ramses, which was situated only a few yards higher on the slope. "It was due to the existence of that tomb that no one violated the tomb of Tutankhamen," he said. "All the rubble from the building operations fell on the young Pharaoh's grave, and it never occurred to later robbers to look beneath so many feet of earth and stone."

Opposite: *The Great Sphinx of Giza and the Pyramid of Chephren*

The boys wanted to visit the tomb of Ramses also. But Gurgar glanced up at the sun and warned that they had no more than half an hour before the first of the swarms of tourists would arrive. "There is just enough time for one of the great royal tombs," he said. He decided on the tomb of Seti I, which Belzoni had broken into with battering rams. That was a most dramatic one, he said. A wide staircase led down into the depths. Light from concealed lamps fell upon the paintings with which the walls of the corridors were covered and brought to uncanny life the figures of winged serpents, demons, all sorts of frightening shapes. The boys made their way into the funerary chambers over wooden planks which bridged deep shafts intended as traps. In the chambers they saw ram-, hippopotamus-, and ibis-headed gods, and one god that was half mummy.

The lofty chamber in which the king had been buried was completely empty. The stone sarcophagus, too, was gone. "Belzoni took it away," Gurgar said. "The robbers had cleaned out all the rest long before."

"I've just been wondering," Achmed spoke up. "If the gold was such a temptation to robbers, why did the Pharaohs want to be buried with it? If they had been buried in just an ordinary way, no one would have troubled to break into their tombs."

"They needed their gold," Gurgar answered, "for very special reasons. I will tell you why."

They were climbing the many steps of the tomb. Once in the open again, Gurgar pointed up to a high peak of the mountain. "I have not been up there in a long time," he said. "Shall we go up there? Then I will tell you about this matter of the Pharaohs' gold."

"Don't you think the hike might be too much for you?" Megdi asked with concern.

"For me?" Gurgar laughed. "For sixteen years I took that path across the mountains every day." Perhaps, however, they all ought to have a snack with him at the small restaurant opposite the tomb of Ramses. Then they would make the climb.

THE ROYAL SECRET

All the way up to the peak not a sound came from the valley. And yet the stillness up here was different from the silence in the tombs; the boys felt that at once. For a long time they sat on their height without saying a word, looking out over the wide valley and the desert. Far below, the Nile sparkled in the sunlight. The fields gleamed, their green sharply demarcated from the stretch of sand out of which arose the barren, rocky cliffs.

"Here, to this place in the West," Gurgar began at last, "all the inhabitants of the Pharaohs' Egypt were brought when their time on earth was over: the poor, the nobles, and the kings. The poor, of course, were simply buried in the sands, though the dry heat of the desert had a curious preserving effect on their bodies. Thus even the lesser folk hoped to have some share in the 'beautiful West.' The privileged classes had provided for their longer future during their lifetimes; they prepared to move into their eternal dwellings in the faith that after death they would again be lords with hosts of servants at their beck and call, ready to make their life as pleasant, stately, and successful as it had always been heir wealth came from the land, so they provided themselves with ands of serfs to till the fields and tend the vineyards. They esteemed pleasure and so they would have dancing girls dancing, nusicians playing. Their spiritual life must also be kept in order, o they had priests bringing sacrifices. Since they regarded the Pharaoh as existing in order to bestow more upon them, the sons f Horus were shown mounting the throne to decree new honours nd riches for them. In fact, the dignitaries of the New Kingdom ad the custom of wearing two golden hearts upon their breasts, to how that the Pharaoh's heart beat for them as well as their own. They wore these same two hearts within their tombs. Accustomed ll their lives to being showered with the blessings of heaven and avours from the king, they unreservedly laid claim to these benefits for eternity.

"What about the Pharaohs, then? We might imagine that since veryone grovelled in the dust before them and all paths were moothed for them, their road to the West would be equally mooth, so that they could travel it without fear. Why, then, were uch horrible images painted upon the walls of their tombs: demons with executioners' swords held in blood-red hands, monsters earful to behold? After all, the Pharaohs themselves decided what vas to appear in their tombs. And the tombs of the Pharaohs differed from those of the nobles, where nothing was pictured but a leasant replica of their fortunate lives. There can be only one explanation: what the Pharaoh awaited was not an everlasting festival, an eternal day without a cloud, but rather a test, a trial of errors, a passage through dark realms in which the mighty ones f the nether world reigned, who were by no means benevolent.

The Pharaohs knew that they would have to pass without flinching through twelve gates, behind which lurked torment and horror. Demons would bar their way; the Pharaohs would have to have great presence of mind, would have to look these demons in the eye, name their antagonists by name and force them to retreat. The way to the West was blocked by hateful shapes; every turn was a trap. After his death, the king had to make his way through twelve hells. And once he had overcome all the horrors, passed through all the terrible gates, there was still a last judgement before Osiris, who had died and been resurrected, and who now sat on the seat of judgement. A dreadful creature lurked behind him, slavering, eager to tear the dead Pharaoh to pieces if the verdict went against him. Forty-two accusers, sent out from every province of the two lands, subjected the departed soul to questioning. He had to aver that he had falsified no measures, neither lied nor slandered nor eavesdropped. A long list of faults and misdemeanours was held up before him like a mirror. The accusers asked: 'Have you ever surrendered to hopelessness?' And woe to the dead soul who could not declare: 'I have not consumed my heart.'

"This heart was then taken out of his breast by Horus and weighed by Anubis. In the other pan of the scales lay a pen, sign of Maat, of heavenly justice, which it was the kings' duty to make a reality upon this earth. If the heart and the pen balanced, Pharaoh would be transfigured, and led by Isis would mount upon the throne of Osiris.

"The Pharaoh was prepared for all this. The pictures and texts which were chiselled into the corridors during his lifetime were meant to remind him that he had already endured these trials

230

once before. During the difficult exercises which he submitted to in the service of the temple, his spirit learned to rise into higher realms. From step to step he was initiated into the secret of dying and coming to new life. In the course of such rehearsals it might happen that the king's body would become rigid as a mummy, as though his spirit had already fled. The king suffered as saints would suffer in moments of ecstasy thousands of years later; he experienced death during life, and learned that death was not an end, but a passage to another life.

"Like the sun which sets only to rise in the morning, Pharaoh at the end of his earthly course descended into the nether world: a Son of the Sun from whose countenance a radiance streamed— that is what the golden mask symbolized—and with fingers that sparkled like rays of light—that is what the golden casings were for. Enclosed in the radiance of the sun, he appeared before Osiris in a coffin that glowed like the barge in which the sun travelled across the sky.

"During their initiation into the mysteries of the religion, the kings had heard the promise of Osiris, first king of the world: 'I was dead and I live—there is no lasting death.' Because of this message countless pilgrims travelled year after year to the tomb of Osiris in Abydos. There they laid offerings, erected memorial stones, and took part in the mystery plays that were given there. In their faith in a last judgement and resurrection, Pharaoh and the meanest porter were equal.

"Sarcophagi have been found with their entire inner surfaces in-scribed with religious texts. The Creator is cited as saying: 'I made the four winds, so that every man might breathe them. I made the

231

waters, so that poor and rich may drink from them. I made every man like his neighbour.' If that were so, then every man could 'descend to the canal and sail to Abydos, in order to travel through the Oldest Land in transfigured form.' Every man could become Osiris at the end. That was the people's hope, and the priests gave each dying man spells to take to his grave with him, although only the initiate understood the full meaning of these spells. The ordinary mortal, too, was provided with the ankh, the sign of life, and with the Eye of Horus which had awakened Osiris to new life. And in place of his heart a scarab was placed on each dead man's chest; he would lay this scarab in the scales, so that his own guilt-laden heart would not weigh them down. In this way the departed soul hoped to find mercy in the Judge's eyes.

"The Pharaohs set out on their way to the West in full aware-ness of the terrors that awaited them. They took weapons with them to be used against the monsters. Tutankhamen set forth on his last journey protected sevenfold by three coffins and four shrines. Neither for the kings nor for the demons was the gold placed in the tombs mere gold. The radiance that shot forth from the gold was not a sign of wealth, but of strength. To the grave robbers gold was no more than a precious metal; to the king it signified a sacred armament whose brilliance made his adver-saries freeze in their tracks. The Pharaoh needed all the gold that he could have in order to light the darkness he had to pass through before he could ascend to the throne of Osiris. That is the royal secret. Not many know it."

"How do you know all this?" Jacob asked curiously.

"From initiates," Gurgar said without hesitation. "They can

ightly be called that, for they have dedicated their lives to the mysteries which lie locked in the temples and tombs of the ancient Egyptians. They are prepared to take the greatest hardships upon themselves in order to probe as deeply as possible into the world of the Pharaohs."

"Do they know much about Tutankhamen when he was still alive?" Achmed asked.

"Not very much," Gurgar admitted. "After his twelve-year search and his additional five years spent studying the finds, Carter said: 'The only thing we know for certain about Tutankhamen is that he was born and died.' "

"That much had been known before," Achmed remarked judiciously.

"It had been known ever since men like Howard Carter came across the name of Tutankhamen in the course of their excavations," Gurgar replied. "Before that, not even the name was known. And Carter's work did of course lead to considerable knowledge. Carter found hundreds, even thousands of objects, and even the smallest had something to tell him. For example, a tiny iron disk amid all the gold amulets in the bandages suggested relations with the people of the Hittite empire, who were making iron weapons and were therefore justly feared by all their neighbours. A memorial tablet turned up in which the young king abjured the god of the heretic Ikhnaton. Inscribed clay tablets, found only a few years ago in Turkey, contained two letters from the youthful widow of Tutankhamen. From such diverse finds, scattered here and there, the initiates can read the story of the young king and his wife Ankhesnamen.

"Tutankhamen was still a child when the country rose up against Ikhnaton and destroyed the city of Aten. He had grown up in this city and had been taught to worship Aten. After Nefertiti's quarrel with her husband, she took this child into her palace, the 'House of Aten,' to which she had sulkily retired. Ikhnaton raised one of his daughters to the throne alongside himself. A young man named Semenkhkare was married to another daughter and became co-regent. Then came the uprising and the Horizon of Aten was razed to the ground. Semenkhkare evidently lost all support, and the powers that be decided that the young Tutankhamen should succeed. The youthful daughter-widow of the dead Ikhnaton was given to the young man for a wife. At the age of twelve the new Pharaoh was a helpless tool in the hands of the men who really held power. They made him move to Thebes and change his name. All the former gods were restored to honour, mightier than ever. Henceforth only the 'sons of someone,' descendants of the families who had ruled before Ikhnaton came to the throne, could become dignitaries. Undoubtedly the person who held the real power at

Scarab: Neb-Kheperu-Ra

udgement of the dead, from a papyrus of the New Kingdom

hat time was General Horemheb, commander-in-chief of the
Egyptian army. As soon as Ikhnaton was eliminated, he began an
nvasion of Palestine to drive back the Khabiru and to impress
upon the peoples of Asia the fact that the god who had the last
vord in Egypt was no longer mild Aten, who had been a father
o all nations, but the old gods of Thebes and their warlike servants.

"Tutankhamen died young, at the age of seventeen or eighteen.
Ankhesnamen, widowed for the second time while still a young
voman, did something altogether unprecedented. She sent a mes-
enger on a secret mission to the king of the Hittites, the most
powerful ruler in Asia, and requested him to send her one of his
ons at once: she would make him her husband and king of
Egypt. The Hittite king was mistrustful; he wanted first to find
ut how things stood in Egypt. In a second letter Ankhesnamen
implored him not to delay any longer since 'she did not want to
ake one of her servants for a husband.' Whereupon the Hittite
king did send a prince. But it was too late. The Hittite suitor never

235

arrived. Meanwhile, the seventy days between the death and the burial of Tutankhamen had passed. Ay, the man who had supervised the entombment of the young king, seized the queen and throne for himself and disposed of the Hittite prince—unless Horemheb did so. In any case, the powerful general, seeing that the hour had struck, had Ay put out of the way—although Ay had been so sure of himself that in the tomb of Tutankhamen he had already had himself represented as king. Raised to the throne of the Pharaohs, Horemheb restored the old conditions with great strictness. He wiped out every reminder of Ikhnaton, and referred to him only as 'that blasphemer.' The end of the great Eighteenth Dynasty came amid the clash of arms. And henceforth military power was to be the decisive factor in the life of Egypt. The kings who came after Horemheb, who are known as the Ramessides, 'made their enemies corpses in the valleys,' as the kings had done in the days before Ikhnaton. Tutankhamen and his hapless young wife had been crushed in this struggle between the god of light and of war. The tool of others during his life, the young king did not even occupy the tomb originally assigned to him. That one was kept by the ambitious Ay, while the four chambers in the rock which Carter discovered were modest ones grubbed out in haste. That much, at any rate, we can detect today. In ten or twenty years, perhaps, we will know considerably more; how much more depends on how many clues the robbers left for the archaeologists.' Gurgar nodded his head in the direction of Qurna. "Some people do not care to help us save these clues."

"They don't understand what it is all about," Jacob burst out. "You ought to tell everyone in Qurna what you have told us."

236

"How often I have tried!" Gurgar said. "But no one ever listened to me—you boys are the first."

Achmed did not reveal what he was thinking. The tension between him and Gurgar could be tangibly felt in the silence. Then Megdi put his hand into his pocket and brought out the little figurine which he had found in the forbidden shaft. Achmed only glanced at it.

"An *ushabti*," he said. "You wouldn't get much for that."

"I wouldn't part with it for ten pounds," Megdi said.

Achmed gave it another, sharper look. "It's nothing special," he declared authoritatively.

"Maybe not for you," Megdi said. "But it is for me!"

"Why?" Achmed wanted to know.

"Because it reminds me of the time I went grave robbing."

"You went grave robbing?" Jacob asked in amazement.

"For one day," Gurgar put in. "Or to be exact, for three hours."

"That's right," Megdi confirmed. "Until I found my answerer." He looked at Gurgar.

"He had all the makings of a grave robber," Gurgar declared with mock seriousness. "Even the courage. He thought nothing of crawling into a shaft that might have collapsed any minute. I was in a cold sweat when I fetched him out of that shaft—that was how dangerous it was in there."

"No, it wasn't," Megdi said deprecatingly.

"It was," Gurgar repeated. "Only you couldn't see how frightened I was because I was crawling in front of you."

"You weren't scared a bit?" Achmed asked Megdi.

"I didn't have sense enough to be," Megdi replied.

"You mean you wouldn't do it again?"

"No," Megdi declared firmly.

"Too bad," Achmed said. "Because I might happen to know a shaft that none of the excavators know about."

"Be careful," Gurgar warned him. "Megdi will be coming back I give you my word that he'll be here again before a year ha passed."

"Maybe I'll write to you," Achmed said to Megdi. "Or Gurgar will write to you for me—keep you in touch with things around here."

Megdi was still holding the small answerer in his hand. "I'd gladly give it to you," he said to Achmed. "Only then I'll have nothing to give to Jacob."

"Give it to me," Gurgar proposed. "Then each of you will have one."

The boys looked at him in astonishment.

"That would be the sensible way," Gurgar said gaily. "I'll have the one that Megdi has. You," he said to Achmed and Jacob, "have me. And you," he turned to Megdi, "have someone who can give you answers better than I can: your father."

"That's not what my father says," Megdi contradicted. "He always says that I cannot learn half as much from him as from you."

"Your father is mistaken," Gurgar protested modestly. Somewhere in the course of this parley he had taken the *ushabti* away from Megdi so skilfully that Megdi did not realize it until he saw his empty hand.

"You'd be a wonderful pickpocket," Achmed said with sincere admiration. Then they began the descent.

Shortly before they reached Sheik Ali's house, Gurgar reached into one of the wide pockets of his *galabia* and brought out a finger-length fish of painted baked clay.

"An Abydos fish," he said. "They are not so common in tombs as *ushabtis*. The ancients believed that the fish swam ahead of the sun during the night to show it the way through the darkness."

"A pretty little pilot," Achmed said warmly.

"Here, give it to Titi," Gurgar said. "Why should she alone come off empty-handed?"

MEGDI MAKES A DISCOVERY

Three months later to the day Megdi went out to Giza again—
visit the forbidden shaft. He had not been as far as the shaft sinc
his first visit, although he had come to meet his father, who wa
still working on the buried ship, fairly often during these pa
months.

Megdi had no thought of climbing into the shaft. Somethin
else entirely had impelled him to come. At home he had found
letter from Gurgar. He had not opened it at once, but decided o
the spur of the moment to read it where he had met the old ma
for the first time.

When Megdi turned off into the desert, the sun had alread
moved away from the Nile toward the pyramids. In an hour or s
it would be time for him to meet Father. Megdi sat down at th
edge of the shaft and took the letter out of his shirt pocket. Care
fully, he opened the envelope which had his name and address o
the front and nothing but Gurgar's name on the back flap. Then I
unfolded the letter—and found himself staring at rows of hiere
glyphics.

Megdi's eyes wandered from sign to sign. Toward the end of th letter he recognized a king's name, that of Seti I. That was all that Megdi could read. At first he was annoyed with Gurgar, then with himself. Finally he decided to look up his father and ask him for help.

Following the same road that he had taken with Gurgar, Megdi walked toward the Great Pyramid. The gaffer at the buried boat waved to him from a distance, and on Megdi's request, set off at once to call Father.

As soon as Father had glanced at the letter, he declared that the matter was too important to be postponed. They climbed up ten or twelve rows of blocks on the south side of the pyramid, where tourists were not allowed. Here they sat down. Opposite them they had the central Pyramid, at their feet the two solar boats, and to their left the Sphinx; but at the moment their attention was fixed upon Gurgar's letter. Father skimmed over the hieroglyphics, while Megdi tried to read his expression.

"Why does he have to write in hieroglyphics?" Megdi grumbled.

"It's a four-thousand-year-old habit with him," Father said as he went on reading.

"But you would think he could write to *me* in the alphabet we learn in school."

"That is asking too much of him," Father defended Gurgar. "He never went to school."

That disposed of Megdi for a while, and Father was able to finish reading the letter. Then he read it aloud: "From Gurgar, Achmed, and Jacob, to Megdi. On the twenty-seventh day of the third month of our friendship. We three hope that you and your father are well. As for myself, I have nothing to write that is worth a letter. I am writing on behalf of Achmed and Jacob. Jacob wishes to ask you

241

whether you still intend to be an archaeologist like your father. Because if so he wants to be what I am and help you some day, as I helped Petrie and Carter. Jacob sends you a promise of this. But Achmed sends you a secret that has been guarded in his family since time immemorial. He has won permission from his father to share the secret with you. Listen, then: In the royal tomb of Seti I, under the sarcophagus, is the beginning of a shaft that leads deep into the mountain. It is a secret corridor that no archaeologist knows about."

"But now *you* know it!" Megdi exclaimed in alarm.

"You can depend on me to keep a secret," Father assured him.

"Wouldn't you have to report anything of this sort?"

"Not in this case."

"Why not?" An uncomfortable suspicion was stirring in Megdi.

Father reflected a moment. "I had better tell you," he said. "The corridor is exactly 303 feet long, but originally it extended deeper. We have not yet penetrated beyond the spot at which it collapsed."

"Then you knew about the passage!" Megdi exclaimed in utter amazement. "And do others know about it too?"

"That is something that ought to please you," Father said. "As an archaeologist. Perhaps you will work on that shaft with Jacob some day." He took Megdi's wrist. "Achmed does not know that we know about the passage. None of the Qurnese know. Think of what that means; we were there first this time. However, this fact does not detract a bit from the significance of Achmed's action. This is something you may well be proud of. Listen to what else Gurgar writes: 'No one in Qurna has ever shared such a secret with me.' "

There was a light veil of cloud over the sky as father and son set out on the way home. They did not take the much-travelled road past the Great Pyramid to Mena House, but went instead down to the canal, passing by the Sphinx. At this hour there were few tourists about. The two went up to the great wedge of rock which had been fashioned into a lion with a human head. At present the stone head was enclosed in scaffolding, but even through the wooden planks it looked enormous and impressive.

"Do you know what the people call it?" the archaeologist asked. *"Abu el Hul*—Father of Terror. The Greeks regarded the great human lion as the protector of the city of the dead, the guardian in the desert. With all that was strange and inexplicable in Egypt, nothing has been puzzled over so much as the Sphinx. And no other monument has so often been rescued from the desert; archaeologists, naval captains, and emperors have fought back the sands. The first to dig out the Sphinx was a Pharaoh. Here may be the oldest excavation site in the world."

Father led Megdi over to the memorial tablet which Thutmose IV had placed there, and read a passage of the text: "And the god spoke to me: 'I am your father, Horu Khutu, the Rising Sun, and will give to you the two lands. You shall wear his red crown and his white crown, and the diadem of the god will shine over you.'" Father smiled. "None of the later excavators were ever rewarded so handsomely for their service."

They looked up at the Sphinx, in whose shadow they stood. The vast and mutilated face rose against the eastern sky. "For five thousand years it has faced the rising of the Sun which signified both the god and Pharaoh," Father said. "It is hard to believe that any people could once have been so unmindful of its dignity as to use it as a target for their cannon." Thoughtfully the two walked on down to the fields, and then along the edge of the desert toward the house of Giza. Megdi's thoughts dwelt on Gurgar, Achmed, and Jacob. It troubled him that he had had to ask his father's help. I cannot even read a letter from Gurgar, he brooded, and the secret shaft is only half a secret. As for discovering anything myself—who knows whether I'll ever come to that. . . .

Megdi glanced up at the pyramids, which now lay to the left. Then he saw something that made him catch his breath. Above the Great Pyramid the thin layer of cloud had broken open. A fan of the sun's rays was falling through the gap—and Megdi noticed something: the outermost rays, which reached from the sky to the earth, fell at the same angle as the sides of the pyramid. Megdi beheld it as a pyramid of light whose concealed apex was the sun. He gripped his father's arm. "Do you see it!" he exclaimed, overwhelmed by the beauty of it. "A pyramid reaching to the sky!"

"The oldest pyramid in the world," Father said.

Suddenly Megdi recalled the mysterious words that Gurgar had read from the walls of the pyramid of Unas: "A ramp of light has been laid under your feet." And suddenly the true meaning of those words was revealed to him.

"You have made an important discovery," Father said.

"But thousands of people must have seen the pyramid of light. . . ."

"Like the head of the Sphinx at Saqqara," Father said. "But the thousands did not give it a thought. Only Mariette had an idea when he saw it—and that made a discoverer of him. Thousands had seen the black millstone in the British Museum with its almost effaced symbols. But only Breasted studied the signs so patiently that at last the stone gave up its secret. Many a sultry summer's day the scholar sat on a stool in front of the stone, flashing daylight on it with a hand mirror until he had made out the age-old text which on orders from a Pharaoh had been transferred from a worm-eaten papyrus to this stone, so that it might be permanent. Centuries later a peasant had used the heavy tablet as a millstone, and had ground away a third of the text. But two thirds had remained legible, and Breasted was able to decipher the earliest thoughts of men which have been transmitted to us in writing. Thus, he discovered one of the most important witnesses to the world of the Pharaohs—far from the Nile."

They turned to go. Suddenly Father said: "I almost forgot to tell you—very soon now we're going to be opening the chamber in which the second buried boat lies. I have obtained permission to bring you along."

"Me?" Megdi asked.

"Why not?" Father said. "After all, you're one of us now."

Sign of infinity

DYNASTIES OF THE PHARAOHS

Under the reign of the Macedonian king Ptolemy II (285-246 B.C.) an Egyptian named Manetho wrote a history of Egypt in which he grouped the Pharaohs, from Menes, the unifier of the two lands, to Alexander the Great, into thirty dynasties. Although quite a few of these groupings seem to lack rhyme or reason, they have nevertheless become established. Recent discoveries and archaeological research have enabled historians to fill in the list of the kings, and to define with more exactitude the length of their reigns. With the exception of the data for the Twelfth Dynasty, for which there is an astronomical coordinate, the dates may be out by some twenty years—in the oldest period by even more. The transition from hunting to agriculture in the Nile valley took place some time in the fifth millennium B.C. This summary follows Dr. von Beckerath. All dates are B.C.

I. THINITE AGE (*First and Second Dynasties*): 2950-2630.

Kings from the Oldest Land, the region around This, succeed in uniting Upper and Lower Egypt. Menes is credited with the building of the White Walls, the capital city later called Memphis. Prime achievements in all phases of civilization; development of writing and the calendar.

II. OLD KINGDOM: 2630-2150.

Third Dynasty: 2630-2580. Imhotep, architect to King Zoser—subsequently to be worshipped as a god, even by the Greeks—builds the first monumental stone structure in the world, the step pyramid of Saqqara. Huni, the last Pharaoh of this dynasty, begins the pyramid of Medum.

Fourth Dynasty: 2580-2465. Snefru, Cheops, Chephren, Mycerinus and others. Building of the great pyramids of Dahshur and Giza. Purest expression of the ancient Egyptian character. Pharaoh as god.

Fifth Dynasty: 2465-2335. Userkaf, Sahure and others build temples to the Sun. Heliopolis assumes a leading role. The first pyramid texts appear in the pyramid of Unas.

Sixth to Eighth Dynasties: 2335-2150. Kings Pepi and Teti. Magical texts in their pyramids also. Queen Nitokris. The nobles and dignitaries become more powerful. Awakening of individual consciousness. Splitting of the two kingdoms; finally, overthrow of all existing values. Social chaos.

Ninth and Tenth Dynasties: (Herakleopolites). First interregnum to 2134.

III. MIDDLE KINGDOM: 2134-1580.

Eleventh Dynasty: 2134-1991. Kings Antef, Mentuhotep and others from the region around Thebes reunite the kingdom.

Twelfth Dynasty: 1991-1785. Kings Amenemhet and Sesostris lead Egypt to new heights of prosperity and civilization. By building a dam they create a fruitful new province in the Faiyum.

Thirteenth to Sixteenth Dynasties: 1785-1580. Second interregnum. Asiatic invaders settle in the delta (Auaris) and subjugate all of Egypt. Time of the Hyksos (foreign rulers).

247

Seventeenth Dynasty: Theban princes, among them Tuyu "whom Ra has made brave," begin throwing off the foreign rule.

IV. NEW KINGDOM: 1580-1085.

Eighteenth Dynasty: 1580-1314. King Ahmose drives the Hyksos farther back. Kings Amenophis I, Thutmose I, and Thutmose II complete the liberation. Having become Pharaoh in her own right, peace-loving Queen Hatshepsut attempts to heal the wounds of foreign rule and long wars. Expedition to the Incense Land of Punt. Under Hatshepsut, Sennemut builds the terraced temple of Dai al-Bahri.

Bellicose Thutmose III founds the Egyptian Empire. Under his successors, Amenophis II, Thutmose IV, and Amenophis III, there is a movement away from Thebes. Amenophis IV completes the break with the old gods and with imperial policies, builds the "Horizon of Aten," and inspires the Amarna period. He calls himself Akhenaten, a name more widely known in the form of Ikhnaton. The beautiful Queen Nefertiti shares the throne with Ikhnaton. In 1338 he is condemned as a "heretic" and his city destroyed. He is followed by Tutankhamen, Ay, and Horemheb, the latter a general who usurps the throne.

Nineteenth and Twentieth Dynasties: 1314-1085. Ramses I-XI, Seti I and II, and other kings. Struggle against the "peoples of the sea." A wealth of building, especially under Ramses II.

V. LATE PERIOD (*Twenty-First to Thirtieth Dynasties*): 1085-341.

Priest kings, Pharaohs from Bubastis, Sais, Ethiopia, Persia, and Macedonia, follow one another until Egypt becomes a province of Rome. Decadence in all spheres of culture, weakening of religion to such an extent that one of the last seers of the Land of the Nile cried prophetically: "O Egypt, Egypt, your religion will be no more than a fable which not even your own children will think true! Nothing but words will remain, hewn in stone, to tell of your acts of piety. The world will be loathsome to man, no longer admirable. Darkness will be preferred to light, and death held more desirable than life. Gods and men will be at odds—to the harm of both—and only the wicked angels will remain. A time will come in which it will seem folly to imagine that Egypt once thought reverence for the divine of greater importance than anything else."

GLOSSARY

Abydos   City in the Oldest Land (the province of This in Upp Egypt). Chief site of Osiris worship, contains royal tombs of t First and Second Dynasties. Behind the temple of Seti I, on a lo lying island, is situated the "Tomb of Osiris."

Amarna   Akhetaten, "Horizon of Aten," the city that Ikhnaton bu in Central Egypt after his break with the gods of Thebes. Now call Tel el Amarna.

Anubis   The god who prepared the deceased for his journey to t "Land of the Western Ones."

Apis   Holy bull, worshipped especially in Thebes.

Aten   The god of the universe, whom Ikhnaton raised above all t other gods.

Auaris   Capital of the Hyksos (the "foreign rulers").

Ba   A name for the soul, frequently represented in the form of a bi

Biban el Muluk   The Valley of the Kings in Upper Egypt (Thebe containing royal tombs of the New Kingdom.

Canopic jars or chests   Vessels in which the internal organs of hi ranking persons were buried after death.

Dai al-Bahri   "Northern Monastery," a gorge in western Thebes c taining the temples of Mentuhotep and Queen Hatshepsut.

Der el Medineh   "Monastery of the City," a settlement for the artis

250

and artists employed in building and adorning the temples and tombs during the era of the New Kingdom.

ragoman (plural *dragomans* or *dragomen*)   Native guides for tourists.

iyum   Large oasis fifty miles south-east of Cairo, connected by a canal to the Nile. A dam erected here by the kings of the Twelfth Dynasty made this area one of the most fertile in Egypt.

ffer   Guard, overseer.

labia   A wide, smock-like garment.

b   God of the earth.

za   Suburb of Cairo, on the edge of the western desert. On a wide plateau stand the pyramids of Cheops, Chephren and Mycerinus, the Great Sphinx, and many mastabas.

pi   God of the Nile.

tnub   "House of Gold," a large alabaster quarry to the south-east of Amarna.

bsed   Anniversary festival and ceremony performed by the Pharaoh for renewal of his rule, usually after thirty years of a reign.

liopolis   "City of the Pillar," or Sun City, situated some seven miles to the north-east of present-day Cairo; it contained an important temple to the Sun, of which only an obelisk remains.

eroglyphics   "Holy Symbols," the script of the ancient Egyptians. Later two derivatives, hieratic (the "priestly script") and demotic (the "popular script"), were developed.

rus   God who was worshipped in the guise of a falcon. As ruler of the earth he was the son of Osiris.

ksos   "Foreign rulers," Asiatic chiefs who conquered Egypt during the period between the Middle Kingdom and the New Kingdom.

s   Sister and wife of Osiris, mother of Horus.

*   The spiritual essence of a human being, which according to the

belief of the ancient Egyptians could enter into the mummy or the statue of a dead person.

Karnak A temple area in eastern Thebes, connected with the temple of Luxor by an avenue of male sphinxes.

Khnemu The god who formed men and gods and their *ka* on his potter's wheel.

Maat The ancient Egyptian concept for order in the world, for truth and justice. At the judgement of the dead, the heart of the deceased would be weighed against the sign of *maat,* a pen. Also, Egyptian goddess of justice.

Mastaba "Bench," the rectangular superstructure of a tomb, characteristic of the Old Kingdom.

Memnon, Colossus of One of the two sixty-foot statues of Amenophis III in front of his mortuary temple in Thebes. The northern colossus had cracked after an earthquake, and from 27 B.C. to A.D. 199 (when it was repaired by the Roman Emperor Lucius Septimius Severus) used to give forth a wailing tone at sunrise. This phenomenon attracted many visitors. The Greeks considered the colossus to be a statue of the legendary Ethiopian king Memnon, who supposedly had fallen at Troy.

Memphis "The White Walls," erected by Menes, the unifier of the two lands, on the border between Upper and Lower Egypt. As the "Balance of the Two Lands" Memphis became the capital of the entire kingdom.

Mortuary temple The temple in which the rites for the deceased were performed.

Mummies Embalmed bodies.

Necropolis "City of the Dead," cemetery.

Nephthys Sister and wife of Set, the brother and murderer of Osiris.

Nut Goddess of the sky who reigned over sun, moon, and stars.

belisk "Roasting spit," gigantic needle of stone which symbolized the sun god whose first rays touched the small golden pyramid upon the apex of the obelisk.

siris The god of the resurrection, at first ruler over all Egypt, later regarded as king and judge in the land of the shades, the "beautiful West."

apyrus A reed, today almost vanished from Egypt, but once plentiful and characteristic of the land. It provided the model for pillars, material for light boats, mats, ropes, sandals, baskets. When fine strips were cut from its pith, laid one upon the other and pressed, an excellent writing paper was produced. These were the famous papyrus scrolls.

haraoh "Great House," the word for the royal palace in the Old and Middle Kingdoms. In the New Kingdom it became synonymous with king.

hoenix Sacred bird, belonging to the sun god.

ah The Creator god of Memphis, represented in human form.

unt The Land of Incense on the coast of the Red Sea, to which expeditions were sent by various Pharaohs, including Hatshepsut.

yramids The Greek designation for the tombs (residences in the hereafter) of kings of the Third to Seventeenth Dynasties. In the New Kingdom modest-sized pyramids were erected even over private tombs. The names of some pyramids: Snefru Appears; Horizon of Khufu; Great is Chephren; Divine is Mycerinus; the Places of Unas are Complete; Everlasting is the Life of Pepi.

urna Village in Upper Egypt which occupies an area thickly sown with some of the most important tombs of the New Kingdom. Towering above it is El Qurn, a pyramid-shaped peak which was regarded as the seat of the goddess Mersegret, "she who loves silence."

Ra Sun god. The Pharaohs from the Fifth Dynasty on regarded them
selves as his sons.

Reis Foreman at excavations, captain on Nile ships.

Saqqara The necropolis of the Old Kingdom at Memphis; its mo
important structure is the Step Pyramid.

Scarab Beetle, symbol of "the god who arises out of himself," cor
mon as an amulet buried with the dead.

Sekhmet "The Mighty One," lion-headed goddess of Memphis.

Serdab "Underground vault," a chamber for the statue of the e
tombed person, with eye-level slits for seeing out.

Set Brother of Osiris, and later his murderer. God of the desert, ov
come by Horus.

Sothis Sirius. The day on which this star first reappeared in the s
shortly before sunrise was celebrated as a great festival. At the beg
ning of historical time this "emergence" marked the onset of t
Nile's flood stage.

Sphinx Image of a king in the form of a lion's body with human hea
With the exception of a few sphinxes of Queen Hatshepsut, m
sphinxes are masculine, but it has been the custom since the ti
of the Greeks to consider them feminine.

Tem The primal god in Heliopolis.

Thebes Capital of the Egyptian Empire, to which the Greeks gave t
epithet "hundred-gated."

Thinites Kings of the First and Second Dynasties; the unifiers
Egypt.

Thoth God of wisdom who taught men to read, write, and reckon.

Uraeus The diadem of the Pharaoh, shaped like a cobra about
strike.

Ushabti "Answerer," a small figure required to serve its master
the hereafter by performing any task to which the master may
called.

AUTHOR'S NOTE

My thanks are due to the Egyptian State Administration of Antiquities, the German Archaeological Institute in Cairo, and the Egyptological Seminar of Munich University, who lent unstinting aid to my researches. I am especially indebted to Professor Hanns Stock, who generously placed his library at my disposal. During my stay in Egypt, Professor Stock, Professor Bakir, Dr. Munro, Mrs. Bolbol el Megdi (Um e Seti), Ibrahim Kemal, and Heinz Herzer were most kind in helping me to find my way about. I wish to thank Professor H. W. Müller for valuable suggestions, and Dr. von Beckerath and Heinz Herzer for looking over the manuscript. The characters of my story grew out of actual encounters in the Land of the Nile. Sheik Ali Abderrasul is a real person, while Megdi and his father are based on an archaeologist and his son, whom I met there. Jacob and Achmed are patterned after boys in Giza, Saqqara, and Qurna.

The coloured plates opposite pages 32 above, 129 below, 144 above, and 192 above are based on photographs I myself took. All other coloured plates have been reproduced from photographs by Albert Burges.

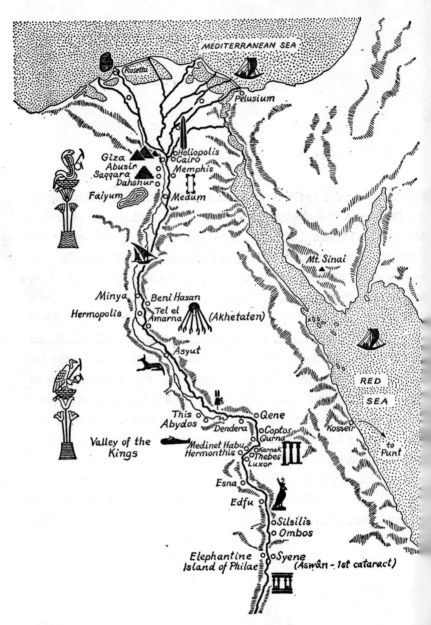

Map of Upper and Lower Egypt. Bottom left, the patron goddesses of the "two Lands": Buto, the cobra goddess (Lower Egypt), and Nekhebet, the vulture goddess (Upper Egypt)

cop 2

F
BAU
BAUMANN, HANS
The world of the Pharaohs

cop 2

F
BAU
BAUMANN, HANS
The world of the Pharaohs

DATE DUE	BORROWER'S NAME	ROOM NUMBER
SEP 28	John Herman	
MAY 3	Sandy Adams	
OCT 1	Tammy Pidsepayl	